"Who punched you out?"

"Teddy! You have a black eye!"

"The first chance I get, I'm gonna cream that kid, you see if I don't!"

"What kid? Who were you fighting with?" Val asked.

"None of your business," Teddy said again. He glanced over at the plate of cookies on the bedside table and snatched one, jamming it into his mouth and munching silently.

Val was trying very hard to keep her temper, but it wasn't easy. "Teddy, you are my brother. If somebody beats up on you, it most certainly is my business. Now I'm going to ask you one more time, and I want a straight answer, or else I'll black your *other* eye! Who punched you out?"

**Look for these books
in the Animal Inn series
from Apple Paperbacks**

#1 Pets are for Keeps
#2 A Kid's Best Friend
#3 Monkey Business
#4 Scaredy Cat
#5 Adopt-A-Pet

ANIMAL INN

SCAREDY CAT

Virginia Vail

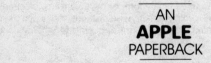

AN
APPLE
PAPERBACK

SCHOLASTIC INC.
New York Toronto London Auckland Sydney

To my friends at Sheepy Hollow

ISBN 0-590-40184-X

12 11 10 9 8 7 6 5 4   8 9/8 0 1 2/9

Printed in the U.S.A.   28

First Scholastic printing, April 1987

Chapter
1

Valentine Taylor trudged into the big stone house on Old Mill Road and tossed her knapsack, softball bat, and fielder's mitt onto the oak bench that stood in the hall. She'd just come from softball practice after school, and she was hot and tired. Even though it was only April, the day had been very warm. Usually, Val would have been working at her father's veterinary clinic, Animal Inn, but now that spring was here, she had to divide her time between Animal Inn and the Hamilton Raiders, the girls' softball team of Alexander Hamilton Junior High in Essex, Pennsylvania. More than anything, Val wanted to be a veterinarian like her father, Doc Taylor, when she grew up, but Doc insisted that she not neglect school activities, and Val was one of the Raiders' star players.

Val sniffed the air. Mmm, something smelled delicious! Mrs. Racer, the Taylors' Mennonite housekeeper, must be baking some of her super-wonderful cookies. Ice cold milk would sure hit the spot right now, too.

On her way to the kitchen, Val picked up Cleveland, her big fat orange cat, and draped him around her neck. Cleveland purred happily. He didn't mind being treated as though he were a fur piece.

"How's it going, Cleveland?" Val asked, rubbing his ears.

Rrrrowww, Cleveland replied, which meant, in cat talk, that everything was fine.

Sunshine, the golden retriever, padded up to Val, tail wagging, and Val leaned down to pat him.

"Where's your pal?" she asked. "Where's Jocko?" Jocko was the Taylors' other dog, a spunky little shaggy black-and-white mongrel. Usually, wherever Sunshine went, Jocko went, too. But this afternoon there was no sign of him. Come to think of it, there was no sign of anybody at all — not Val's younger sister Erin or her little brother, Teddy. The house was surprisingly quiet.

Val went through the dining room into the kitchen. Mrs. Racer was just taking a tray of cookies out of the oven.

"Hi, Mrs. Racer," Val said, putting Cleveland down on the butcher block table. "Those cookies look as good as they smell. I'm starved! May I have some? I promise it won't spoil my appetite for supper."

2

Mrs. Racer's bright blue eyes sparkled in her flushed face as she smiled at Val. "Sure, you can. I know it takes more than a few cookies to spoil anybody's appetite in this family. But wait a few minutes till they cool off, or you'll burn your tongue. There's plenty of milk in the refrigerator, if you're thirsty."

"Am I ever!" Val grinned and headed for the refrigerator. "Where is everybody?" she asked, taking out the frosty pitcher.

Mrs. Racer handed her a glass. "Erin went over to Olivia's after ballet class. She'll be home at six. And Teddy . . . well, Teddy's upstairs in his room."

That surprised Val. Teddy never went to his room unless he was sick or getting ready for bed.

"Is he all right?" she asked. Ever since her mother's death over three years ago, Val had shared with Mrs. Racer the responsibility for her youngest brother and sister. Doc Taylor, her father, tried to make sure that Val led a happy, normal life, but Val couldn't help worrying about Teddy and Erin.

"Well, he is and he isn't," said Mrs. Racer, frowning. "Tell you the truth, Vallie, I don't know what's wrong with him, but *something* is, that's for sure. You know he's been acting kind of funny lately. . . ."

Val nodded. Impish, mischievous eight-year-old Teddy had been very quiet these past few days, and that wasn't like Teddy at all. "Maybe he's coming

3

down with something," she suggested. "Did you take his temperature?"

"Nope. Couldn't catch him," sighed Mrs. Racer. "He came home after school and ran right upstairs. Took Jocko with him, and shut himself in his room. He didn't even ask to lick the cookie dough out of the bowl, and I'd saved it for him special."

"He *must* be sick," Val decided. "I'll take some cookies up to him and try to find out what's wrong."

Mrs. Racer piled several cookies on a plate while Val drank her milk. Then Val took the plate and, followed by Sunshine and Cleveland, went out of the kitchen and up the stairs. She stopped in front of Teddy's door and knocked briskly.

"Teddy? It's me, Vallie. Can I come in?"

"No. Go away!" Teddy answered. His voice sounded muffled, as though he had his head buried in a pillow.

"I have cookies," Val said. "Fresh out of the oven. Your favorite — peanut-butterscotch-choco-late chip."

"I said go away!"

He's sick, all right, Val thought. She'd never known Teddy to turn down an offer of Mrs. Racer's cookies before.

"Teddy, I'm coming in," she said. "If I don't, I'll have to give these cookies to Sunshine, and that would be a terrible waste."

"Don't care," Teddy mumbled. "Don't bug me, Vallie. I mean it!"

But Val opened the door anyway and came into the room. She found her little brother lying face down on his bed. Teddy didn't look up when Val entered. Instead, he grabbed a pillow and plopped it on top of his head. Val went over to the bed, put the plate of cookies down on the bedside table, and sat next to Teddy.

"What's wrong?" she asked, reaching out to rub his back. But Teddy pulled away from her hand, mumbling something she couldn't hear. Jocko, who had been lying under the bed, scrabbled out to greet Val—and the cookies. "No, Jocko, they're not for you," Val said sternly. "Go chase Cleveland or something."

Jocko scampered off, cheerful as always, and settled himself under Teddy's bed again. Val turned her attention back to Teddy.

"Is it a tummy ache?" Val asked.

No answer.

"Sore throat?"

Nothing.

"Flunk a test?"

The head under the pillow shook back and forth.

"Then what's the matter? If you don't tell me, how do you expect me to help you?" Val asked, beginning to get annoyed.

"Don't want help. Don't need help. Go away!" Teddy muttered.

"At least *look* at me when you talk to me," Val said, snatching the pillow away.

Teddy immediately covered his face with both hands. He struggled like mad when Val tried to pull his hands away, but since she was bigger and stronger than he, she succeeded. When she saw his face, she let out a little squawk.

"Teddy! You have a black eye!"

He certainly did — only "black" wasn't the right word to describe it. The skin around Teddy's right eye was swollen, and an amazing shade of purple.

"Boy, you're real smart, Vallie. How'd you figure that out?" Teddy growled, looking daggers at her with his other eye. "So I have a black eye! So what? Now will you go away?"

"No, I certainly will not!" Val snapped. "How'd you get it? You were in a fight, right? Who with?"

"None of your business," Teddy said, picking up his beloved Phillies baseball cap, which had fallen on the floor, and jamming it down over his golden-brown curls so that the visor cast a shadow over the injured eye.

"It is too my business!" Val told him. "Who started it? You or the other guy? You know how Dad feels about fighting. He's going to be very upset."

"I'm kinda upset, too, in case you hadn't noticed," Teddy said. "And the first chance I get, I'm gonna *cream* that kid, you see if I don't!"

"What kid? Who were you fighting with?" Val asked.

"None of your business," Teddy said again. He glanced over at the plate of cookies on the bedside table and snatched one, jamming it into his mouth and munching silently.

Val was trying very hard to keep her temper, but it wasn't easy. "Teddy, you are my brother. If somebody beats up on you, it most certainly is my business. Now I'm going to ask you one more time, and I want a straight answer, or else I'll black your *other* eye! Who punched you out?"

Teddy swallowed his mouthful of cookie, then washed it down with a drink of lemonade. At last he said, "You don't know this kid. Sparky just moved to town about two weeks ago."

"Someone in your class?" Val asked.

"Yeah." Teddy took another cookie. "And everybody hates Sparky already. That kid's the biggest bully in the whole school!"

"What did you fight about?" Val took a cookie, too.

"Well, Eric and Billy and me were playing *Star Wars* at recess, and it was my turn to be Darth Vader. And then Sparky comes up and says, '*I'm* gonna be Darth Vader.' And Eric says, 'No, you're not. You're

7

not gonna be anybody. Get lost!' And then Sparky shoved Eric, and grabbed my Darth Vader sword — it was really a stick — and I grabbed it back, and that's when Sparky punched me in the eye," Teddy said. "And then Mrs. Reinhart — she's the play-ground monitor — she came over and took Sparky and me to the principal's office. And Mr. Stauffer blamed *me* for the whole thing! He said I oughta know better than to pick on a new kid, and he said he's gonna call Dad and tell him. It's not fair! All I did was kick Sparky in the shins. It only made a little, tiny bruise."

"That doesn't sound fair, all right," Val agreed. "But you're going to have to tell the whole story to Dad. I'm sure he'll understand that it wasn't really your fault."

"Maybe I'll run away," Teddy muttered, pulling his cap further down over his eyes. "Maybe I'll go to California or something. I really *hate* that kid!"

Jocko, who had been under the bed the whole time, wriggled out and jumped up next to Teddy, licking his face.

"How'd you like to go to California, boy?" Teddy asked, putting his arm around the dog. "I bet you'd like it fine."

"Teddy, you are *not* going to California," Val said sternly. "You're going to stay right here and work

8

things out with Sparky. He's probably okay once you get to know him. I bet he's just lonely, in a new town and a new school and all, with no friends."

"Well, Sparky's not going to make any friends, either," Teddy said. "The only thing Sparky's gonna make is *enemies* — lots of 'em!"

Val sighed. "I'm going to make an ice pack to put on your eye. It will bring down the swelling. Then you can take Jocko for a walk, and Sunshine, too. You can't just stay in your room."

"Oh, yes I can," Teddy told her. "If I go out, somebody might see me, and they'll laugh themselves sick!"

"Why?" Val asked, puzzled. "What's so funny about a black eye?"

"Because Sparky gave it to me, and Sparky's a. . . ." Teddy stopped dead.

"Sparky's a what?"

"Nothing," Teddy mumbled. "Forget it."

"Oh, for heaven's sake!" Val sighed. "Come on down into the kitchen — I'll fill the ice bag and you can watch TV with your good eye for a while. Mrs. Racer's worried about you, and you don't want her to worry, do you?"

"No, I guess not," Teddy said. "C'mon, Jocko — let's go. I'll take you and Sunshine for a walk after it gets dark."

"Wow, look at that shiner!" Erin cried as she caught sight of Teddy's eye. She had sat down on the floor beside him to watch television, but the black eye had caught her attention right away. "Wait till Daddy sees. He's going to have a fit."

"Shut up, Erin, okay?" Teddy said, scowling. "Just leave me alone."

"*Excuse* me," Erin said, raising her eyebrows. "Excuse me for *living*!" She flounced out into the kitchen, where Val was helping Mrs. Racer by cutting out baking powder biscuits. "What happened to Teddy? Did he get into a fight?" she asked. "He's in a terrible mood."

"He sure is," Val agreed. "The best thing to do is to leave him alone. He got into a fight with a new kid in school, and they were hauled into the principal's office. Teddy's mad because Mr. Stauffer said it was all his fault."

"Honestly!" Erin said indignantly. "How could it be Teddy's fault that he got a black eye? Unless he pulverized the other kid, that is."

"He says he didn't," said Mrs. Racer. "Sounds to me like this new boy, this Sparky, is a real big bully. I'm going to tell Doc he ought to go to your school first thing tomorrow morning and talk to the principal himself. Our Teddy's not a bad boy. He never gets into fights — well, hardly ever. Erin, make yourself useful. Here's a baking sheet. You can put Val's biscuits on it and put it in the oven."

"*Val's* biscuits?" Erin echoed. "Vallie, did you make the dough?"

"Nope. Mrs. Racer did. I'm just cutting them out," Val said.

"Thank goodness!" Erin sighed. "The last time you made baking powder biscuits, they were a disaster. You forget to put the baking powder in! Even the dogs wouldn't eat them."

"Thanks for reminding me," Val said acidly. "I may not be much of a cook, but even *I* can't ruin Mrs. Racer's biscuits. Come on, Erin. Fill that baking sheet."

"Yes, boss. Right away!" Erin said with a grin. "Where's Daddy? It's after six — isn't he home yet?"

"Not yet," Mrs. Racer said, "You know how it is this time of year. What with lambing, and calving, and foaling, spring's just about the busiest season for Doc. He called and said he had to go to Mr. Bauer's farm to help his prize ewe. Seems she's having trouble birthing — he thinks the lamb's turned around the wrong way."

"Oh, dear," Val said. "I hope she's going to be all right. Rats! I wish I could have gone with him. And I would have, if I hadn't had softball practice this afternoon."

Erin wrinkled her nose. "Lambs are cute when

11

they're little. The problem is that they grow up to be *sheep*, and sheep are awfully dumb."

"Not all sheep are dumb," Val said quickly. "Flossie's pretty smart. And she has such lovely, thick fleece. The Bauers shear their sheep themselves, and Mrs. Bauer cards and spins the wool into the softest yarn. Her daughter makes beatiful sweaters out of it, and sells them. I think sheep are nice."

"I like a nice lamb chop myself," Mrs. Racer said. Then, noticing Val's horrified expression, she added, "Sorry, Vallie. I know how you feel about eating meat. I shouldn't have said that."

"That's all right, Mrs. Racer," Val said. "I don't expect everybody to feel the way I do about animals. Even Dad eats meat, and he loves animals every bit as much as I do."

The faint honk of an automobile horn sounded from in front of the house, and Mrs. Racer quickly took off her spotless white apron, handing it to Erin. "That's m'son, Henry. I have to go. Now, Vallie, you tell Doc that he has to see that Mr. Stauffer at the school right away. We can't let some big bully keep hurting Teddy. Erin, put those biscuits in the oven right before dinner. Ten minutes, no more, or they'll burn."

She hurried out to get her coat. As she passed Teddy, she leaned down and patted the top of his head. "Don't you feel bad, Teddy," she said. "Your eye's going to be fine in a couple of days, just you wait and see. It wasn't your fault that that big bully beat you up."

"Thanks, Mrs. Racer," Teddy said. "But Sparky's not all that big, not really. Just tough, that's all. Next time, I'm gonna punch out all that kid's *teeth*, that's what I'm gonna do!"

Mrs. Racer paused and shook her head. "That's not the way to behave, Teddy," she said. "You're supposed to forgive your enemies, not hurt them when they hurt you."

Now it was Teddy's turn to shake his head. "No way! I'm never going to forgive that kid, not if I live to be as old as you are!"

Mrs. Racer couldn't help laughing. "I'm sixty-five, Teddy. You have a long, long way to go!"

The horn honked again.

"I'll see you tomorrow," Mrs. Racer said. "And mind you keep that ice pack on your eye."

She left then, and Teddy turned his attention back to the television screen. Val could almost hear him thinking: He'd never forgive Sparky, not ever. Not even if he lived to be a hundred and twelve!

13

Chapter 2

Doc Taylor came home half an hour later. He looked tired but pleased.

"Hi, Dad," Val said, giving him a welcome-home kiss on his bearded cheek. "How's Flossie Bauer? Are she and the baby okay?"

Doc grinned and gave her a hug. "Mother and twins are doing just fine," he said.

"*Twins*! Really? Oh, Dad, can you take me out to the Bauers' farm to see them?" Val cried. "Imagine — twin lambs! I wish I'd been there."

"Twins? Mr. Bauer's sheep had twins?" Erin came bouncing into the room and kissed her father. "They must be adorable."

"They're pretty cute, all right," Doc agreed. "I told Mr. Bauer I'd drop by later in the week to check up on them. You can both come with me, if you like." He glanced down at Teddy, who was still sitting in front of the television, his baseball cap pulled way down. "You, too, Teddy. Don't you have a hug or a kiss for your old man?"

Teddy waved, not raising his head. "Hi, Dad."

Doc looked over at Val, raising his eyebrows in a silent question. Val shrugged. "You'd better ask Teddy," she said, but Erin cut in right away.

"Daddy, wait till you see Teddy's eye. He got into a big fight at school today, and he had to go to the principal's office," she announced cheerfully.

"Blabbermouth!" Teddy growled, scowling at his sister.

Doc squatted down next to Teddy and gently lifted the visor of his cap. He let out a long, low whistle. "That's quite a shiner you have there, son. Want to tell me about it?"

"No," Teddy admitted, "but I guess I have to, right?"

"Right," Doc said. "Suppose you and I go up to my study and you can tell me the whole story. Girls," he added to Val and Erin, "this shouldn't take long. Let's eat at seven." He put his arm around Teddy's shoulders and steered him in the direction of the hall stairs. "Now, young man, I want to hear exactly what happened."

At supper that night, Teddy had very little to say. After Val and Erin put the dishes in the dishwasher and cleaned up the kitchen, Teddy took the dogs for their evening walk. Erin went down into the basement to practice some new steps she had learned in ballet class, and Val and Doc went out back to feed Val's rabbits, Archie the duck, and Teddy's chickens.

"Are you going to punish Teddy?" Val asked, pouring pellets of rabbit food into four matching bowls.

Doc shook his head. "No — I think he's been punished enough. And from what he tells me, I'm convinced he didn't start the fight." He checked the water level in the chickens' pan and added a little more. "What I *am* going to do is call the school and make an appointment to speak with Teddy's teacher and the principal. From what I can make out, this Sparky character is a real menace. The fight with Teddy was only one of a number of incidents ever since Sparky joined Teddy's class. He sounds like a real tough customer. If his parents don't know what's going on, someone needs to tell them, and it should come from someone at the school, not another parent."

Val gave a little sigh of relief. "I'm glad you're not going to punish him," she said. "It really wasn't his fault. I just wish I could get my hands on Sparky! Teddy's been miserable lately. He was even talking about running away."

"I know," Doc said. "He told me that, too, when I said I was going to talk to his teacher. But our Teddy has a good head on his shoulders. I'm sure he wouldn't do anything as foolish as that. And I'm sure that I can straighten this whole thing out. In the meantime, I've told Teddy to steer clear of Sparky, particularly at recess. That seems to be when all the trouble starts."

Val picked up Cottontail, the big gray rabbit, and stroked her soft fur. "I wonder what that kid's real name is?" she said.

"Beats me," Doc said. "I asked Teddy several times, but he wouldn't tell me — either that, or he doesn't know. As a matter of fact, he wouldn't tell me anything about Sparky at all except that he's the biggest bully in the third grade and everybody hates him. I can't help feeling sorry for the child, in spite of everything. He's obviously having a hard time adjusting to a new school and a new home."

"I know," Val said. She put Cottontail down and patted Flopsy, Mopsy, and Sam so they wouldn't feel neglected. "But if he wants to make friends, he's sure going about it in the wrong way!"

"Indeed he is," Doc agreed. "Come on honey — let's go back to the house. I'm sure you have home-work to do, and I have some reading to catch up on."

Val made a face. "Yep — I have a social studies report due day after tomorrow, and I'm only halfway through. Dad," she added as they walked side by side through the darkened yard, "will you really take us out to see Flossie's twins?"

"Sure will," Doc promised. "But probably not

until Sunday afternoon. Maybe we can spend a little time at the Bauers' farm. Mrs. Bauer is very eager to have some young visitors — their niece is staying with them for a while, a little girl about Erin's age. From what Mrs. Bauer tells me, Marcy is very lonely. Maybe she and Erin will hit it off."

"That would be nice," Val said. "But I don't see how anybody could be lonely, living on a farm. Even if you didn't have any people-friends, there are all those animals to pal around with."

Doc smiled and ruffled her hair. "Not everybody is as animal-crazy as you are, Vallie. Marcy grew up in Pittsburgh — the only pet she ever had was a canary, and Mr. Bauer says she's terrified of cows, sheep, and even the dog and the barn cats."

"Imagine that!" said Val. "Imagine being *afraid* of animals. Well, at least she and Erin will have something in common. Erin can tell her all about *her* canary." Then she asked, "When we go, can Toby come, too? I bet he'd like to see the lambs. The Currans don't have any sheep on their farm."

Toby Curran, Doc's other young assistant, lived on a dairy farm. Toby was Val's second-best friend, next to Jill Dearborne. Val sometimes thought Toby was a bit too much of a know-it-all when it came to animals, but most of the time they got on together very well.

"As a matter of fact, Toby helped me deliver the

18

lambs this afternoon," Doc told her. "He's turning into a first-rate veterinary assistant."

Val's face fell. "Better than me?" she asked softly. She couldn't help feeling a little jealous.

"No, Vallie, not better than you," Doc assured her warmly. "Nobody could possibly be better than you. But when you're not around, he does his best to lend a hand."

Val relaxed. Her father's good opinion meant more than anything in the world to her. "Well, can he come anyway?" she asked. "Even though he's seen them already?"

"Of course he can, if his folks say it's all right," Doc said. "Now you go right upstairs and dig into that social studies homework."

"Okay, Dad." Val scooped up Cleveland, who had come to greet them at the back door, and went up to her room. Cleveland hopped out of her arms and settled himself on the foot of her bed. Val sat down at her desk and opened her social studies book. She'd study for an hour, then take her shower, tuck Teddy and Erin in for the night, and go to bed herself. Val stifled a yawn. If she could keep her eyes open that long, that is.

"Dad's taking us out to see the lambs on Sunday," Val told Erin later that night as she plumped up her sister's pillows. "And he says the Bauers' niece is staying with them, and she's about your age."

"Really? What's her name?" Erin asked.

"Marcy. She has a canary," Val told her.

"I wonder if she takes ballet lessons," Erin said thoughtfully.

"Maybe she does," Val said. "Dad didn't say. She lives in Pittsburgh."

"Then what's she doing staying with the Bauers?" Erin asked.

"Search me. I didn't ask," Val told her. "Guess I was thinking too much about Teddy. Hey, Erin, you don't know anything about that Sparky kid, do you?"

Erin picked up one of her favorite ballet books from the bedside table and settled herself against her pillows. "*Really*, Vallie. I'm in sixth grade. I don't pay any attention to those little children in third. I wasn't even in the schoolyard at recess. We were rehearsing our class play in the auditorium. It's based on A *Midsummer Night's Dream* — that's by Shakespeare, you know."

Val nodded. "Yes, Erin, I know."

"We're not doing the whole thing — Mrs. Garfield cut it down to forty-five minutes. I'm Titania, the queen of the fairies."

"Yes, Erin, I know," Val said again. For the past two weeks, the Taylor family had heard all about the play and about Erin's role. "And Mrs. Garfield is letting you make up all the dances."

20

"I bet you *don't* know that a long time ago, Moira Shearer played Titania. She was a very famous English ballerina with the most *beautiful* red hair. She's the star of *The Red Shoes*, my absolute most favorite movie ever!"

"I know, I know," Val sighed.

"There's a picture of her as the Swan Queen in *Swan Lake* right here, on page fifty-two," Erin said, flipping through her book. When she reached the page, she shoved it under Val's nose. "Isn't she beautiful? But she's not as beautiful as Mommy was when *she* danced it."

"Nobody was as beautiful as Mommy," Val said softly. Their mother had been a ballet dancer before she'd married Doc. Erin, who had been only eight when Mrs. Taylor died in an automobile accident, was very much like her. Val, on the other hand, resembled Doc and Teddy was a combination of both their parents.

"I'm just going to read for a little while," Erin said. "I'm really pooped. Oh, Vallie, would you cover Dandy's cage? I forgot, and I'm too comfortable to get out of bed again."

"Okay. Lights out in fifteen minutes, Erin. Goodnight, sleep tight. . . ."

". . . don't let the bedbugs bite," Erin finished, smiling. "See you in the morning. And make sure Cleveland goes out with you. Every time he looks at

21

Dandy, I know he's thinking about a snack."

Val draped the cover over the canary's cage, then shooed Cleveland out of the room, closing the door behind her. Next she went to Teddy's room. She found her little brother playing with his favorite hamster, Ringo, while he held the ice pack over his eye with one hand.

"Teddy, put Ringo back with John, George, and Paula," Val said. "You'll get him all excited, and then he'll run in his wheel all night."

"He will even if he *doesn't* get all excited," Teddy said, but he carefully picked up the little animal and carried it over to its Habitrail. "Night, guys," he said. "Try to keep the noise down, okay? A man's gotta get some sleep."

He hopped back into bed and handed the ice pack to Val. "How does my eye look?" he asked anxiously. "Do you think it'll be all better by tomorrow?"

"Well, not *all* better," Val said, "but better, anyway. It'll take a few days for it to stop being purple, but the swelling is definitely going down." She tucked in his sheets and blankets as Teddy rummaged under his pillow and brought out Fuzzy-Wuzzy, the stuffed bear that he always slept with.

"Vallie. . . ." Teddy began, then stopped.

"What?"

"I guess you couldn't ask Dad not to talk to my

22

teacher and the principal tomorrow, huh?'' he asked.

"I could, but it wouldn't do any good," Val told him. "Besides, I'd think you'd be glad he's going. If Miss Vickers and Mr. Stauffer get on Sparky's case, I'm sure he'll stop picking on you. And don't you want Mr. Stauffer to know it really wasn't your fault?''

Teddy groaned. "You don't understand *any-thing*, Vallie! If Dad talks to Miss Vickers and Mr. Stauffer, he'll find out . . . well, he'll find out something about Sparky, and I don't want him to!''

"What will he find out?'' Val asked. "What's the big mystery about Sparky, anyway? Does he have two heads or something?''

"Don't be dumb, Vallie! It's *worse* than that. And when Dad finds out, I'm really gonna get it,'' he said.

Val was completely lost. "I give up. Go to sleep, Teddy. Everything will look better in the morning. It always does.'' She leaned over and kissed his cheek. "Good-night, sleep tight. . . .'' She waited for him to complete the sentence, but Teddy just stuck out his lower lip and clutched Fuzzy-Wuzzy tighter. ". . . don't let the bedbugs bite,'' she said at last. "I'll leave your door open a crack. Dad'll be in to say good-night in a few minutes.'' She was on her way out the door when Teddy spoke.

"Vallie?''

"Yes?''

23

"Promise me something, okay?"

"Sure. What is it?"

"Promise that you won't laugh at me when you find out — what Dad's gonna find out tomorrow," Teddy said.

"*What* is Dad going to find out?"

"Just promise. You promised you'd promise, so if you don't promise, you broke your promise," Teddy said.

"Teddy, you know something? You are really weird sometimes," Val said with a sigh. "Okay. I promised I'd promise, so I promise."

"G'night, Vallie."

" 'Night, Teddy."

As Val left Teddy's room, she met Doc in the hall.

"You look puzzled. What's up?" Doc asked.

"I don't exactly know," Val confessed. "Teddy just made me promise that I wouldn't laugh at him when you find out what you're going to find out about Sparky tomorrow, and I can't imagine what it could be."

"That makes two of us," Doc said. "Maybe Sparky's not a *big* bully, but a *little* bully. If a boy smaller than Teddy blacked his eye, I can see why Teddy might be embarrassed."

"I bet that's it," Val said. "But even if Sparky's only two feet tall, I promised I wouldn't laugh, so I won't. I guess that's why Teddy's afraid you'll be mad — because he knows it's wrong to fight with anybody, but specially with kids littler than he is."

"We'll cross that bridge when we come to it," Doc said. He gave Val a good-night kiss, and went into Teddy's room.

Val got into bed, Cleveland curled up at her feet, and picked up the book she was reading for the third time, *My Friend Flicka*. But every now and then, a picture would flash into her mind of Teddy having a fistfight with a boy who wasn't much bigger than Jocko, and in spite of herself, it made her giggle.

Chapter 3

"Wait till you see the Bauers' twin lambs," Toby said to Val. It was the next afternoon, and Val had biked to Animal Inn as soon as school was over. Toby was holding down a nervous young Doberman pinscher named Gretel while Val tried to persuade the pup to stick her head through a plastic bucket with the bottom cut out. Once the bucket was positioned around Gretel's neck, Val would tie it securely in place. Then Gretel wouldn't be able to scratch at her ears, which had just been cropped and neatly bandaged by Doc. But Gretel didn't want to put her head into the bucket. It was almost as though Gretel knew how silly she'd look, Val thought.

"I'll see them on Sunday," Val said. "Dad's taking Erin and Teddy and me out to the Bauers' farm for a visit. Want to come?"

Gretel scrabbled wildly and whined, trying to escape.

"Hang onto her, Toby. I almost got it that time," Val added. "There, there, Gretel, it's going to be all right. If you'd just sit still for a minute, it would all be over."

Gretel rolled her eyes and whined some more, but she sat still just long enough for Val to pop the bucket over her head. "That's a good girl," Val crooned, deftly tying the cords around the dog's neck. She stroked Gretel's gleaming coat as the Doberman began to calm down.

"Sure. I'd like to come," Toby said. "Can I let her go now? Or is she going to have a fit?"

"I think she'll be okay," Val told him. "Poor pup! I hate it when dogs have their ears cropped. Tails, too. It doesn't seem right that people chop off parts of animals just to make them look different. When I'm a vet, I just won't do it, that's all."

"Then you're going to miss out on a lot of business," Toby said. "The way I see it, it's kind of like plastic surgery in people. If somebody has a big, ugly nose, or ears that stick out a lot, it makes them feel better about themselves when they have them fixed."

"Well, *your* ears stick out a lot — I mean, they kind of stick out a *little*," Val added hastily, "and *you* wouldn't have plastic surgery, I bet. And besides, people make their own decisions about things like that. Poor dogs, like Gretel here, don't have any choice. Maybe she liked her ears the way they were."

"But if she had floppy ears and a long tail, Mrs. Fisher wouldn't be able to enter her in those fancy dog shows," Toby pointed out. Then he grinned. "I guess if I was a dog, I wouldn't win any prizes, either, not with my big ears!"

Val giggled. "They're not all that big," she said. "You can bring Gretel out to Mrs. Fisher now." She handed the dog's leash to Toby. He snapped it on to Gretel's collar.

"Come on, Bucket-head," he said cheerfully. "Let's make tracks."

"Toby!" Val cried. "Don't call her that. You'll hurt her feelings."

"Gimme a break!" Toby sighed. "She doesn't know what I'm saying."

"I wouldn't be so sure," Val said. "I think animals understand a lot more than most people know."

"That's because you're an animal nut," Toby said over his shoulder as he led Gretel into the waiting room. "You're not like 'most people.' "

"Good!" Val replied. "If I was, I wouldn't be a very good vet."

The door closed behind Toby and Gretel, and Val went to help Doc with his next patient. It was a pet pigeon with a broken wing.

"Oh, Walter. What happened to you this time?" Val said, holding the bird gently but firmly while Doc got the X-ray machine ready. "Seems like you were just in here with an infected beak. How'd you hurt your wing?"

Doc handed her a protective apron to guard her from the rays. When Val had put it on, she held Walter in place while the X ray was taken.

"Since Walter doesn't seem about to tell you," Doc said, "I will. Walter got into a fight with one of the neighbor's cats. Fortunately for him, the cat had been declawed, and somehow Walter avoided having his head bitten off, but his wing was broken in the struggle. As soon as I check the picture, I'll set it. Walter will have to stay here for a few days so we can keep an eye on him. Better ask Toby to prepare a cage for him, Vallie."

"Okay." Val handed the pigeon to her father and took off the apron. "Speaking of fights, Dad, did you talk to Teddy's teacher today about Sparky?"

"Yes, I did," Doc said. "First thing this morning. Miss Vickers told me that I was the fifth parent who'd complained so far this week. Teddy's not the only one who has problems. Both Miss Vickers and Mr. Stauffer have had conferences with Sparky's mother. They're thinking about putting the child in a special class for difficult children."

"Difficult! More like impossible if you ask me," Val said. "Maybe you ought to let Teddy stay home until they straighten that kid out."

Doc shook his head. "No, Vallie. We won't solve anything that way. The teacher, the principal, and Sparky's mother are all aware of the situation.

I'm sure it will be taken care of. In the meantime, Teddy stays in school. Now how about telling Toby to fix up that cage? And you can tell Mr. Felton that we'll take care of Walter's wing, and that Walter will have to stay at Animal Inn for a little while. I'll call him when he can pick him up.''

Val did as she was told, then assisted Doc while he set the pigeon's wing. After the last few patients in the waiting room had been taken care of, Pat Demp-wolf, Doc's receptionist, went home. Val helped Toby clean up. When they were finished, Toby hopped on his bike and headed for the Currans' farm, and Val went into the barn to say hello to her big dapple gray horse, The Gray Ghost. Val thought he was the most beautiful horse in the world. And he was extra-special because Val had saved his life by buying him from his owners. They were going to have him put to sleep because he was old and was slowly going blind. The Ghost greeted her with whickers of pleasure.

Val put her arms around his strong, glossy neck and gave him a big hug.

''Hi, Ghost,'' she said, scratching between his ears. ''Miss me?''

The horse snorted and butted his head against her chest. Val laughed and stroked his velvety nose. ''I know what you want,'' she said. Turning her back to him, she bent down and took out an apple from her knapsack. ''Let's see how smart you are,'' she added. Hiding an apple in one hand, she stretched out both fists to the horse. "Okay — which hand has the treat?"

The Ghost snuffled first at one hand, then the other, and began nibbling delicately at the one that held the apple.

"You're smart, all right," Val told him affectionately, offering it to him on her outstretched palm. "You may not be able to see very well, but there's nothing wrong with your nose!" After that, she gave him a second apple and a handful of carrots, patting him while he munched.

"Got any leftovers, Vallie?" asked Mike Strickler, Animal Inn's night man. He was just coming on duty. Val hadn't heard him enter the barn. Now she looked up and smiled at the wiry little old man. She was very fond of Mike. He was as much of an "animal nut" as she was herself.

"A few carrots. Why? Hungry?" she teased.

"Nope — just had a real good supper. Chicken pot-pie at Rose's Diner. Now don't you make a face, Vallie. Just because you don't eat meat doesn't mean the rest of us is cannibals," Mike said, grinning. "I been eating meat all my life, and I'm healthy as this horse here. Yep, been eating meat all my life, and I'll be a hundred-and-twelve my next birthday."

"Oh, Mike!" Val groaned. "*Nobody's* a hundred-and-twelve!"

"Some folks is," said Mike cheerfully. "Now, I might have missed a year or two, come to think of it. Maybe I'll be a hundred-and-thirteen."

Val giggled. "Come on, Mike. How old are you really?" She, Teddy, and Erin had been trying to find out Mike's age ever since he'd started to work for Doc, but he would never, ever tell them.

"That's for me to know and you to find out," Mike said, grinning.

Val handed him the rest of the carrots. "Here. Who're you going to give them to?"

"That poor little heifer two stalls down is feeling mighty lonely. Got no other calves to talk to. Besides, that ringworm she's got makes her feel ugly. I figured a treat might cheer her up some."

"Yes, I feel sorry for her, too," Val said. "I wish I could pat her or something, but ringworm's as contagious to humans as it is to other cows. Be careful you don't catch it, Mike."

Mike snorted. "Don't you think I know how to take care of myself around sick animals? Been doing it ten times as long as you been alive."

"That would make you more than a hundred and *thirty*," Val pointed out with a grin.

"You're right," Mike said. "Guess I'm not quite as old as all that. Hey, Vallie, I forgot to tell you — your dad's lookin' for you. He's ready to go home."

"I guess I'm ready, too," Val said. She turned

back to The Ghost and gave him another hug. " 'Night, Ghost. See you tomorrow. We'll go for a ride, if it isn't raining. 'Night, Mike."

Val hurried out of the barn. Doc was waiting for her in the van. A light mist was falling. Val saw that Doc had put her bike in the back of the van, so she climbed in beside him.

"Wonder how Teddy made out today?" she said as Doc pulled out of the Animal Inn parking lot.

"Better, I hope," said Doc. "We'll find out when we get home."

But when they arrived at the big stone house on Old Mill Road, a worried Mrs. Racer met them at the door.

"Doc," she said, "Teddy didn't come home after school. That's not so unusual, but no matter where he goes, he's always home by around five o'clock. It's after six, and there's no sign of him."

Doc frowned. "Did you call Eric or Billy?"

"I sure did," said Mrs. Racer. "They hadn't seen him since school let out. But Billy said Teddy and Sparky had another fight today in gym class, and Teddy was real upset."

"Maybe he really *did* run away," Erin put in. She was perched on a step halfway down the stairs, her chin in her hands. "Daddy, you've just got to do something about that Sparky kid!"

"It looks as though I'll have to, since nobody else seems to be able to do anything," Doc said grimly. "But the most important thing right now is to find Teddy."

"You don't really think he ran away, do you, Dad?" Val asked.

"Not to California," Doc said, "but I wouldn't be surprised if he's hiding out somewhere closer to home. Val, Erin, it's time to send out a search party, and you're elected. I'll call Eric and Billy again. Maybe Teddy's turned up there. Wait till I talk to them."

But neither Eric nor Billy had any more information. They gave Doc the phone numbers of some of Teddy's other friends, but nobody had seen Teddy in hours.

"All right, girls," Doc told Val and Erin. "Start scouting out the neighborhood. I'll wait here in case Teddy phones."

A car horn honked outside.

"Oh, dear — that's m'son, Henry," said Mrs. Racer. "I'll have to be going. That poor little boy! Maybe something terrible has happened to him. Maybe he got kidnapped or something. You read about things like that happening in the paper all the time. Why, just the other day, there was this little girl. . . ."

"Mrs. Racer, calm down," Doc said sternly. "There's no sense getting yourself into a tizzy. I'm sure Teddy is perfectly fine, and when he comes home, we'll let you know, I promise."

"Oh, all right," Mrs. Racer sighed. "But don't forget. I won't have a moment's peace until I know Teddy's safe and sound at home."

"We promise, Mrs. Racer," Val said, giving her a hug. "I'll call Henry myself."

The horn honked again.

"Oh, dear! Now where's my pocketbook? I declare, I'm so *ferdudtzed* I don't know which way to turn!"

Erin found Mrs. Racer's purse, Val handed her her coat, and Doc escorted her to Henry's car.

"Let's go, Erin," Val said. "I'll take this block — you take the one between Second and Maple. I'll meet you at the corner of Maple in about fifteen minutes."

Erin pulled on her jacket, pulling the hood over her head. It was still raining a little. She sprinted off down the street, and Val headed for the back yard. Maybe Teddy was hiding in the tree house, or in the garage.

He wasn't.

Val then walked up and down both sides of Old Mill Road, peering into yards and under bushes. She would have asked if anybody had seen Teddy, but no one was outside. Everyone was indoors, having their supper. Val was beginning to get really worried. She knew her little brother's appetite. No matter what, he never, ever missed a meal. The fact that it was suppertime and Teddy still hadn't come home meant that something was very wrong.

When she met Erin a few minutes later, Erin had nothing to report, either.

"You don't think that maybe Mrs. Racer's right, do you, Vallie? I mean about Teddy being kidnapped?" she asked.

"Of course not!" Val snapped. "Don't be ridiculous." Then she added more kindly, "I'm sorry I bit your head off, Erin. I'm worried, too, but I honestly don't think anything like that has happened. I think it's more likely that Teddy's just had it up to here with Sparky, and run away."

"Well, how far could he get unless he took some money with him?" Erin said. "We should have checked his piggy bank. He told me the other day that he'd saved up close to ten dollars. Maybe we ought to go back to the house and find out if he took the money."

"Good idea," said Val. The sisters started jogging back home. "Ten dollars wouldn't get him very far, though — maybe to Harrisburg on the bus."

When they got back to the house, however, Doc told them that he'd thought of the same thing and had found Teddy's piggy bank full of nickels, dimes, and quarters. But his sleeping bag was missing, and so was his cub scout mess kit, and Fuzzy-Wuzzy, his bear.

"I take that to mean that Teddy's camping out somewhere," Doc said. "Perhaps he took off for Forest Park. The cub scouts camped there one weekend last fall. Come on, girls — let's take the van to the park. It's as logical a place as any to look."

"Can we bring Jocko and Sunshine?" Val asked. "They're not exactly bloodhounds, but I bet they'd be able to sniff him out if he was anywhere nearby."

"Good idea," Doc said. "I hate to leave the house in case he should call, but since he hasn't phoned by now, I doubt he will. Get the dogs, Vallie. Erin, take one of Teddy's jackets from the hall closet. Wherever he is, he's bound to be getting pretty wet."

Moments later, Val, Erin, Doc, Jocko, and Sunshine were in the van, heading across town toward Forest Park. (Cleveland had wanted to come, too, but Val had explained to him that, with the dogs gone, he had to stay home and act as a watch-cat.)

Suddenly Erin shouted, "*Stop!* Daddy, stop the van!"

Doc did, with a screech of brakes. "What on earth's the matter?" he asked.

"Over there — that vacant lot." Erin pointed. "They're building a new house, see?"

Val gave her sister a puzzled look. "So what? Why did you make Dad stop?"

"Yes, Erin, what's up?" Doc added.

"I just remembered," Erin said. "That's the place

where Teddy and his friends have been playing after school, after the workmen go home! They play war in the foundations — Teddy told me about it the other day." She glanced over at her father. "He told me not to tell you, because he was afraid you wouldn't let him do it anymore because you'd say it was dangerous, only he said it isn't, not really."

"He's right — I would have," Doc said. "You should have told me anyway. But do you think Teddy might be holed up in there?"

"I bet he is," Erin said, getting out of the truck. "C'mon, Vallie! Let's go check it out."

Val hopped out after her, followed by Jocko and Sunshine. The dogs galloped ahead, and Jocko began to bark frantically, stopping by the edge of the foundation and peering down into the cellar of the new house. His tail was wagging. Sunshine joined him and began to bark, too.

Val heard a familiar voice say, "Go away! Get out of here, dogs! How'd you find me, anyhow?"

Val and Erin crouched down beside the dogs. It was pretty dark, but not too dark for them to see Teddy's small figure down below.

"Teddy Taylor, you come out of there right now!" Val commanded, her relief at finding him making her voice sound sharp. She didn't know if she wanted to hug her little brother or to knock him into the middle of next week.

"Daddy's waiting in the van," Erin added.

"No! I'm never coming out!" Teddy said. "You can't make me, either. I'm never going back to that old school, not unless Sparky moves away. I hate that kid, and I hate school, and I'm gonna stay here for the rest of my *life!*"

"Teddy, there's a chicken roasting in the oven at home," said Doc, coming up behind his daughters. "I smelled it the minute I came in the door. And mashed potatoes, and I wouldn't be surprised if there was something special for dessert — like brownies and vanilla ice cream."

"Brownies? Mrs. Racer made brownies?" Teddy's voice sounded weak — with hunger, Val imagined.

"Big, *fat* brownies," she said. "Just the way you like them, with lots of walnuts. If you don't come home with us, we'll never be able to eat them all. We'll have to feed them to the dogs."

There was a scrabbling, scrambling noise in the shadows of the cellar. A moment later, Teddy emerged, dragging his sleeping bag and cub scout mess kit. Fuzzy-Wuzzy was tucked securely under one arm.

Val took the sleeping bag, Erin grabbed the mess kit, and Doc picked up Teddy and Fuzzy-Wuzzy.

"Come on, son. Time for supper," he said gruffly. "And after that, it's time for us to have a serious talk."

Chapter 4

The next morning, Doc, Teddy, and Erin headed for Jackson School in the van. In spite of Teddy's protests, Doc had announced that he was going to speak to Miss Vickers and Mr. Stauffer and insist that something be done about Sparky. He was also determined to talk to Sparky, though Teddy begged him not to.

"It'll just make things worse, Dad," Teddy had said as he scuffed, slow as a snail, toward the van. "Honest it will. Don't you believe me? Couldn't we just move to Alaska or someplace? I bet they need vets up there."

"Teddy, we are not moving to Alaska or anywhere else," Doc said. "We are going to stay right here and settle this Sparky situation once and for all. Now stop dragging your feet and get moving." He turned to Val, who had accompanied them to the driveway. "Vallie, make sure you don't forget to call Pat and tell her I'll be late. If necessary, have her reschedule my early morning appointments for later

40

in the day, and tell her to apologize to anyone I've inconvenienced. I'll see you at Animal Inn after school."

"Okay, Dad," Val said. "Cheer up, Teddy. Everything's going to be fine, you'll see."

"You don't understand," Teddy sighed. "*Nobody* understands!"

"*I* sure don't understand," Erin said. "If it was me, I'd be happy that Daddy was going to stand up for me. I don't know what's the matter with you."

Teddy didn't reply. He just climbed into the van and sat there scowling, looking as though he'd lost his best friend.

Val watched them drive away, shaking her head in bewilderment. Erin was right. Teddy was acting really weird about this whole thing. But if anyone could straighten things out, Doc could, she was sure.

When Val arrived at Animal Inn that afternoon, Doc told her that he had seen both Teddy's teacher and the principal. A conference had been set up with Sparky's mother for next Monday morning. It would be decided then whether Sparky would be allowed to remain in Teddy's third grade class, or be removed to the "special" class.

Since there were very few patients waiting to be seen and Toby was there to help Doc for a while, Val took The Ghost out for a short ride, then rubbed him down and let him out into the pasture behind the Large Animal Clinic. When she returned to take up her duties, Pat told her she had to leave early because it was her granddaughter Tiffany's third birthday, and Tiffany's mother was having a party. Val sat down at the reception desk and began taking calls. Val wasn't exactly crazy about answering the phone. She'd much rather have been taking care of Doc's animal patients, but she knew she had to pitch in whenever she was needed.

Rrrring!

Val picked up the phone. "Good afternoon. Animal Inn. May I help you?"

"Uh . . . yeah, I guess so. Can I talk to the vet?"

It was a child's voice, and the voice sounded worried.

"I'm sorry — Doctor Taylor is treating a patient right now," Val said. "If you'll tell me what's the matter, I'll give him the message."

"Oh."

Silence.

"Uh . . . well, it's my cat, Charlie. He's sick."

"What are his symptoms?" Val asked, pulling a note pad closer to her and picking up a pen.

"He looks awful!" The child's voice sounded close to tears. "I came home from school, see, and Mrs. Wilson — that's our housekeeper — she told me that Charlie didn't look good. And he didn't eat

42

his breakfast or anything. She said he just lay there all day, and now he's breathing real funny, and there's lots of gooky stuff coming out of his eyes, and . . . and I think he's gonna *die*! Can the doctor come over right away and look at him?''

Val frowned, writing down everything she'd heard. ''Not right now, I'm afraid,'' she said. ''Like I said, he's busy with a patient. Can you bring Charlie to Animal Inn?''

''No!'' the child wailed. ''Mrs. Wilson doesn't have a car, and my mom's at work. And I'm not allowed to go on the bus by myself. And even if I was, I don't know what bus to take. We just moved here a few weeks ago. But Charlie's real sick! He needs to see a doctor right away. Can't Doctor Taylor come here? My mom'll pay. She has a real good job. She has plenty of money, honest.''

''Give me your name and address,'' said Val. ''Doctor Taylor will come over as soon as he's free.''

She heard a gusty sigh of relief. ''Okay. I'm Phil Sparks, and I live at 713 Walnut Street. How long do you think it'll be before the doctor can come?''

Sparks? Val's ears pricked up. It couldn't be — could it? ''Sparks, you said?'' she asked. ''Is that S-P-A-R-K-S? Like in *Sparky*?''

''Yeah, that's right,'' the child said. ''But the name under the doorbell is Alison Sparks. That's my mom. My dad doesn't live with us. He and my mom got divorced last year. He lives in York. He's gonna get married again. When do you think the doctor'll come to see Charlie?''

"Just as soon as he's through with his other patients," Val replied. "Listen — uh — Phil. . . .''

"Call me Sparky. Everybody does."

I can't believe this! Val thought. It has to be the same kid! Getting herself together, she said, "Sparky, where do you go to school? We have to have information like that for our records," she added hastily.

"Jackson. I *hate* that school! Those kids are really mean. I wish my mom and dad hadn't got divorced. Divorce is the *pits*, 'cause if they hadn't been divorced, I'd still live in York and go to my old school. I had a lot of friends there. But I don't have any friends in Essex. I bet Charlie wouldn't have gotten sick if we still lived in York. He had a lot of cat friends, too. Maybe that's why he got sick. He misses his friends."

"Yeah — maybe so." Val could hardly believe her ears. She was actually talking to the dreadful, terrible Sparky! "Look, Phil — uh, Sparky — I'll give Doctor Taylor all the information, and he'll come to your house as soon as he can. In the meantime, keep Charlie quiet, and offer him milk or water to drink if he doesn't want to eat anything. And if he doesn't want to drink, either, give him water with an eyedropper. If he doesn't drink anything, he might go into convulsions."

"Okay, I'll do that," Sparky said. "But he doesn't seem to want to eat or drink anything. His nose is so clogged up that he can't smell. I opened a can of anchovies this afternoon — Charlie loves anchovies — and he didn't even look at them. I guess that's because he can't smell them, right?"

"Right," Val said. "Just keep getting fluids into him. Doc Taylor will be there in about an hour."

"Gee, thanks!" The child sounded a little more cheerful. "I guess maybe Charlie's just got a bad cold, huh? And if it's only a cold, he won't die, will he? I get colds all the time, and it's no big deal, right?"

"That's right," Val replied. "We'll be there in about an hour. I'm Doc Taylor's assistant. I'll be coming with him."

"Okay. See you in about an hour. Only please hurry!"

"We'll be there as soon as we can."

Val hung up the phone. "Well, I'll be darned!" she said aloud, to nobody in particular.

"What's up?" Toby asked, pausing by the reception desk. "You look funny."

"I *feel* funny," Val admitted. "You'll never guess in a million years who that was on the phone!"

"No, I won't unless you tell me," said Toby patiently.

"It was *Sparky*, that's who!" Val cried.

"Sparky? Who's Sparky?" Toby asked.

"Honestly!" Val sighed. "The kid who's been beating up on my little brother. You remember — I told you all about him."

"Oh — *that* Sparky. Are you sure?"

"How many Sparkies can there be who just moved to town and go to Jackson School? Of course I'm sure. His cat's sick, and Dad and I are going over there as soon as Dad's free. I can hardly wait!"

"What're you going to do to him? Poison his cat?" Toby joked.

Val frowned. "Toby, that's not funny. We'll take care of his cat — it sounds like he's really sick. Sparky sounded real worried. And a kid who cares so much about his pet can't be all bad. . . ."

"Maybe that cat's sick because the kid beat up on him, too," Toby suggested.

"You don't get a runny nose and gooky eyes and lose your appetite because someone beat you up," Val told him. "No, I'm sure Sparky's scared about his cat. It sounds like Charlie's his only friend. I guess Charlie *is* his only friend — Sparky sure hasn't made any other friends since he came to Essex."

"You didn't answer my question. What are you gonna say to him? Are you gonna tell him to stop making Teddy's life miserable?" Toby persisted.

"You bet I am!" Val blustered. "And Dad will, too."

But she couldn't help remembering the real fear

and sorrow in Sparky's voice. Somehow the idea of coming face to face with the third grade bully in a situation like this wasn't very appealing. She had to admit that she felt sorry for Phil Sparks. But, she reminded herself, she felt a lot sorrier for the cat.

"Answer the phone if it rings, will you, Toby?" she asked. "I have to tell Dad that he has a house call to make."

"So this is where the Third Grade Terror lives," Doc said as he parked the Animal Inn van in front of 713 Walnut Street. It was a neat brick house with three stone steps leading up to a front door painted dark green. There was almost no front yard, but a gate at one side opened onto a path that ran along to what appeared to be a big back yard.

As he and Val got out of the van, Val asked the same question Toby had asked her. "What are you going to do, Dad?"

"You mean about Teddy? I haven't decided," Doc said. He stepped up on the stoop and pushed the doorbell. "First, we attend to our patient. That's the reason we're here. We'll worry about Teddy's problem later."

Val nodded.

Just then a short, stocky woman opened the green door. "Yes?" she said, looking from Doc to Val. Then she saw Doc's black bag. "Oh, you're the vet, aren't you? Come right in, Dr. Taylor. I'm real glad you're here. Phil's worried to death about that poor cat." She glanced at Val. "Who're you?"

"This is my daughter, Val. She's also my assistant," Doc told her before Val could speak. "Where's the patient?"

"In the kitchen. Follow me, please. I'm Mrs. Wilson, the housekeeper. Phil's keeping Charlie company. Right this way."

Doc and Val followed Mrs. Wilson into the kitchen. Val noticed that there were still some unpacked cartons standing against the wall. Apparently the Sparkses were not completely settled in.

"Phil, the doctor's here," said Mrs. Wilson.

Val's eyes widened as a sturdy little figure stood up and came toward them. Shiny brown hair formed two stubby braids, each tied with a bright red ribbon. There was a sprinkling of freckles across the bridge of a small, pert nose, and huge brown eyes gazed at Doc, fringed with thick, dark lashes. The little girl was wearing a blue T-shirt and faded jeans. Small, scuffed sneakers were on her feet.

"*Sparky?*" Val gasped.

"Yeah, that's me. And this is Charlie." The child pointed to a wicker cat bed on the kitchen table where a large gray and white cat lay on a pink corduroy cushion. The cat's eyes were closed and it was breathing rapidly and shallowly.

"But . . . but you're a *girl!*" Val managed to say.

"I know," Sparky said, watching Doc. "You're going to make Charlie well, aren't you, Dr. Taylor? He's my best friend. He's not gonna die, is he?"

"I certainly hope not, Sparky," Doc said. He put his bag down on the table next to the wicker basket. "Vallie, hold the cat. I'm going to examine him now. My, he's a fine big fellow, isn't he?"

"But, Dad, Sparky's a *girl!*" Val repeated.

"So she is," Doc replied. "Interesting, isn't it? Vallie, are you going to hold that cat or not?"

"Yes — yes, sure." Val gently lifted Charlie from his basket so Doc could take a good look at him. Her thoughts were whirling. Now she understood why Teddy had been so unwilling for anyone to find out more about Sparky. It was bad enough being beaten up by the new *boy* in school, but a girl . . . ! His classmates must have teased the daylights out of him, Val imagined. No wonder he wanted to run away to Alaska!

Sparky stood beside Doc, clasping her hands tightly in front of her. "See all that junk running out of his eyes?" she said. "We keep cleaning it out, but it keeps on coming. And he's breathing so funny. Sometimes it's like he's not breathing at all. He's not very old. He's almost exactly as old as me. I'm eight. Cats live lots longer than that, don't they?"

"Yes, they do," Doc said, lifting one of Charlie's

49

eyelids and peering into a cloudy yellow eye. "Especially cats like this one — big, strong cats. We have a cat at home — this is my daughter, by the way. Her name's Valentine, but everyone calls her Val, or Vallie. Cleveland — that's our cat — is her special pet. I bet Cleveland is almost as big as Charlie, isn't he, Vallie?"

"Uh — yes. Yes, I guess he is," Val said. She couldn't stop staring at Sparky. "What's your real name?" she burst out. "You said your name was Phil when I talked to you on the phone. But that's a boy's name."

Sparky's face became very pink. "It's not my real name. I'm like you."

Val frowned. "What do you mean?"

"Well, your name's Valentine, but people call you Val or Vallie. My name's . . ." Sparky swallowed hard, ". . . Philomena. Only everyone calls me Phil. Or Sparky. I like Sparky better. Back in York, everybody called me Sparky. They call me that here, too. Only back in York, they liked me. Nobody likes me in Essex. But that's okay, because I don't like anybody in Essex, either!"

"Why don't they like you, Sparky?" Doc asked, opening Charlie's mouth and looking down his throat.

"Because I fight a lot." Sparky shoved the end of one pigtail into her mouth and chewed on it. "Do you know what's wrong with Charlie?"

50

"Not yet, but I'm going to find out soon. Vallie, I want to take a blood sample. Give me a syringe, please."

Val took one out of the black bag and handed it to her father. While he filled it with Charlie's blood, Val stroked the cat's head. Its ears were burning up with fever and its pink nose was hot, too. She glanced up at Doc, worried.

"Yes, I know," he said. "Charlie's running quite a fever." He turned to Sparky. "My daughter told me that Charlie only got sick today, is that right?"

"That's right," said Mrs. Wilson, who had been hovering in the background during the examination.

"He looked okay when I left for school this morning," Sparky said. "Well . . . he *looked* okay, but he didn't eat his breakfast, only I thought that was because I'd given him a big snack before we went to bed last night. Chicken livers. He loves 'em and I hate 'em."

"But during the day, he got worse and worse," Mrs. Wilson put in. "Sparky, stop chewing on your hair. You know your mother doesn't like you to do that."

Sparky removed the wet pigtail end from her mouth. "I know," she sighed. She reached out and stroked Charlie's thick gray fur, and her eyes brimmed with tears again. "You oughta see Charlie when he's well," she said, in a choked little voice. "He's real

51

playful. And when I give him a new catnip mouse, he just goes crazy."

"So does my cat, Cleveland," Val told her, smiling. "He'll be well again, you wait and see. Doc's the best vet there is." Even though she now knew that this was the Third Grade Terror, as Doc had put it, she felt so sorry for the little girl that it didn't matter anymore. The only thing that mattered was curing Charlie and making Sparky smile.

"Where is your mother, Sparky?" Doc asked. He put the syringe containing the blood sample into his bag and pulled out a hypodermic filled with antibiotic.

"She's at work," Sparky said. "Like I told Val on the phone, she has a real good job. She's a para . . . para. . . ."

"Paralegal," Mrs. Wilson supplied. "Mrs. Sparks works for Haskins, Lebo and White over on Pomfret Street. She'll be home in about half an hour."

"Yeah, that's right," Sparky said. "She's like a lawyer, only she's not exactly a lawyer. She helps all those lawyers do their work. She went to school to learn how to do it. Maybe I'll be a lawyer when I grow up."

"Good for you, Sparky," Doc said. "Now here's what we're going to do for Charlie. I'm going to give him a shot of antibiotic, and Val will give you a bottle of medicine for him. You or Mrs. Wilson must give him half a dropperful three times a day. Keep trying to get fluids into him, and offer him his favorite food every now and then — *not* anchovies. They're too salty. But don't worry if he doesn't want to eat. Charlie's fat enough to do without eating for a few days. Then tomorrow afternoon, I want your mother to call me at Animal Inn to set up an appointment. I'll have the results of the blood test by then, and I'll know exactly what to do for Charlie.''

"Should I give him nose drops?" Sparky asked. " 'Cause his nose is still all stuffed up."

"No, better not," Doc told her. "People nose drops are too strong for a cat's delicate tissues. It would only irritate Charlie's nose and make him feel worse. In the meantime, just give him plenty of love and make sure he gets his medicine on schedule."

Val handed Sparky a small bottle filled with pink fluid. "Half a dropper, no more," she reminded the child.

"Okay." Sparky nodded. Then she looked up at Doc. "Doctor Taylor, he *is* gonna get better, isn't he? He isn't gonna die? If Charlie dies, I don't know what I'll do. He's the only friend I have left!"

Doc stroked the top of Sparky's head, as though she were a frightened little animal in need of soothing. "We're going to do our very best for him, Sparky. That's a promise. I can't tell you more than that. Charlie's a big, strong cat, and it's obvious that you love him very much. Love is sometimes almost more important than medicine in making an animal get well. Now don't forget to have your mother call me tomorrow." He shook Mrs. Wilson's hand. "Nice meeting you, Mrs. Wilson. Take good care of this young lady and my patient," he said. "Vallie, we'd better get going."

Val snapped Doc's black bag closed and picked it up.

" 'Bye, Mrs. Wilson. See you tomorrow, Sparky, and Charlie, too. And remember — my dad's the best vet there is, so don't worry."

Mrs. Wilson showed Val and Doc out. Sparky stayed beside Charlie's basket, patting him and talking to him softly.

As they got into the van, Val said, "Dad, that cat's got me worried. It isn't just a bad cold, is it?"

Doc shook his head. "No, I'm afraid it's not."

"Are you thinking what I'm thinking?" Val asked softly.

"Suppose you tell me what you're thinking, and I'll let you know," Doc said with a faint smile.

"Feline leukemia," Val said.

Doc heaved a sigh. "I'm afraid that's exactly what I'm thinking, Vallie. And if that's what the tests show, Charlie's chances of recovery are very slim indeed."

Chapter
5

In the van on the way home, Doc and Val agreed that, for the moment anyway, they wouldn't say anything about meeting Sparky.

"The less said in this case, the better," Doc told Val. "Tomorrow's Saturday, so there's no danger of Teddy having another run-in with Sparky then. And by the time Monday rolls around, I will have had a talk with Mrs. Sparks — and possibly Sparky as well. Considering how upset Sparky is about her cat, I think I'll handle it instead of talking to the school again."

"Poor kid," Val sighed. "She may be tough on the outside, but inside, she's a real marshmallow. I know exactly how she feels about Charlie. I'd be torn to pieces if Cleveland came down with feline leukemia."

"We don't know that's what it is," Doc reminded her, "and Sparky doesn't even know it's a possibility. Besides, Cleveland has been immunized. Drat!" he said suddenly. "I was so surprised at the transformation of the class bully into a scared little girl with pigtails that I completely forgot to ask if Charlie had had all his shots. Well, we'll find out tomorrow. It's better that Sparky not have something else to worry about."

"A lot of people don't even know that there *are* shots to make sure their cats don't get it," Val said sadly, "even though any good vet should have sent out cards to all his patients when the vaccine first was available. We did."

"Pet owners don't always follow through on things like that, Vallie." Doc said. "They tend to think that something as serious as leukemia is very rare, and there's very little chance that their cat will come down with it. Unfortunately, that's not the case." He drove the van into the driveway beside the Taylors' house. "Well, here we are. Remember — not a word to Teddy, or Erin, or even Mrs. Racer. We paid a house call on a sick cat. No need to go into details."

Val nodded. "I'll keep quiet. Oh, Dad, is it all right if I go over to Jill's after supper tonight? She asked me to sleep over. It's okay with her folks. I meant to ask you before, but the sight of Sparky knocked it right out of my head — just like you with the shots."

"Yes, Vallie, it's all right."

They got out of the van and headed for the front door.

"Can I tell Jill about Sparky?" Val asked before

they went in. "She wouldn't tell a soul, honest. And I have to tell *someone!* It's just too big a secret to keep all to myself."

Doc hesitated, then said, "I suppose so. But whatever you do, don't tell Teddy."

"Don't tell Teddy what?" shouted Teddy, coming up behind Doc and giving him a big hug around the waist.

Doc grinned down at him. "Curses! Foiled again! Guess we have to tell him, Vallie."

"We do?" Val gasped, staring at her father. Was he going to tell after all?

"Yep, we do. Or rather, *I* do. I was going to keep it a secret, but now I guess I'll have to let everybody know — I'm going to take all of you to Curran's Dairy Store for ice cream after supper tonight. Jill, too, if she'd like to come."

"I bet she'd love it!" Val cried, and Teddy said, "Can Billy come, too?"

"I don't see why not," Doc said. "An ice-cream pig-out for all the Taylors and special friends."

"Boy, I think it's neat that Toby's dad has an ice cream parlor," Teddy said happily. He raced ahead of them to tell Erin, and Val glanced up at her father.

"Dad, you told a *lie*," she whispered.

Doc cocked an eyebrow at her. "A very small one, Vallie, and only to keep the peace, and to save Teddy from embarrassment. And come to think of it, it's not really a lie, because I *was* going to take all of you for ice cream after supper, Sparky or no Sparky."

Val laughed. "Okay. Then it doesn't really count, does it?"

"Not at all," Doc said, putting an arm around her shoulders and giving her an affectionate hug.

After their ice-cream treat at Curran's Dairy Store, Val and Jill went to Jill's house, where they talked for hours, then watched a movie on the VCR until they both dozed off. Jill was fascinated to learn that the mean little kid who had been giving Teddy such trouble was actually a girl and sorry to hear about Sparky's sick cat. Jill was still asleep the next morning when Val got up, dressed, and hurried off to Animal Inn on her bike. On Saturdays, she worked a full day, and this Saturday promised to be an especially interesting one. She couldn't wait to find out the results of Charlie's tests, and was immediately saddened when Doc told her that the tests showed that Charlie had tested positive for feline leukemia.

"But you know, Vallie, that if a cat survives the first infection, he has about a thirty-five per cent chance of recovery," Doc told her. "Because Sparky called us right away, Charlie may just make it."

"Oh, I hope so!" Val said. "He's such a big, beautiful cat. And Sparky loves him so much. She'll be miserable if he dies."

"There were no messages on the answering machine from the Sparks family," Doc said, "and if Charlie had taken a turn for the worse, I'm sure either Sparky or her mother would have called. Let me know the minute Mrs. Sparks phones. I want to see Charlie as soon as possible."

Mrs. Sparks called mid-morning to make an appointment, and Val juggled some of Doc's regular patients to make room for Charlie so he wouldn't have to wait any longer than was absolutely necessary. At one o'clock, Sparky arrived at Animal Inn, lugging a big cat carrier, and followed by a tall, slim woman with shoulder-length brown hair.

Val leaped up from behind the reception desk. "Hi, Sparky! How's Charlie doing?"

"Not so great," Sparky said. Her round, freckled face was solemn, and she looked up at her mother, then back at Val. "He slept on my bed all night, and I kept waking up all the time to see if he was still breathing. Sometimes it seemed like he wasn't, but then I poked him, and he made funny little noises. But he didn't eat anything at all."

"None of us got much sleep last night," Mrs. Sparks said, smiling faintly. "I ended up in Philomena's bed, with Charlie wedged between us. Charlie snores just like a person."

"I'll go get my dad," Val said. "Have a seat. I'll be right back."

She ran into the treatment room, where Doc and Toby were finishing up with a sorrowful-looking elderly bassett hound.

"Dad, the Sparkses are here," she said.

"I'll be there in a minute," Doc told her. "Toby, you can take Duke out now. And remind Mr. Frantz about his special diet. No bones. Then you can cover the reception desk while Vallie helps me in here."

"Okay, Doc," Toby said. "C'mon, fella. Right this way." He led Duke by his leash into the waiting room and handed him over to his owner, glancing curiously at Sparky and her mother. He did a double-take, then whispered to Val, "*That's* the tough little kid who's been beating up on Teddy?"

Val nodded and whispered back, "Tell you about it later." To Sparky and Mrs. Sparks, she said, "The doctor will be with you right away. She crouched down in front of Charlie's cat carrier and peered through the mesh, meeting Charlie's big, cloudy yellow eyes. "Hi, Charlie. How ya doing?"

Charlie looked at her. His eyes were covered with a misty film. He opened his pink mouth and mewed very faintly. At least he was still alive!

"Taylor," said Mrs. Sparks, watching Val. "You're not by any chance related to Teddy Taylor, are you?"

Val kept her eyes on Charlie. "Teddy Taylor's my brother," she said.

"I see." Mrs. Sparks looked down at her hand-

60

bag. "Sparky's teacher told me that Teddy's father was not happy about what had happened between Sparky and Teddy. I'm not happy, either."

Val felt uncomfortable. "Uh . . . maybe you better wait and talk to my dad," she said.

"Maybe I'd better," Mrs. Sparks said.

"Teddy's related to the vet?" Sparky said, staring at her mother. "Terrible Teddy's Doctor Taylor's *son*?"

"That seems to be the case," said Mrs. Sparks. "And please don't call him 'Terrible Teddy,' Philomena."

"Geez!" Sparky muttered. She glared at Val. "Why didn't you tell me?"

"What good would it have done?" Val answered. "It wouldn't have made Charlie get better any faster. Dad and I were pretty surprised when we found out who *you* were, too. But Dad didn't want to say anything right away. The important thing is to get Charlie well."

"Geez!" Sparky said again, and stuck the end of a pigtail in her mouth.

"Philomena . . ." said her mother, and Sparky took the pigtail out.

"Sorry, Mom."

Doc came into the waiting room just then. "Hello, Sparky," he said. "Mrs. Sparks? I'm Doctor Taylor."

Mrs. Sparks stood up to shake his hand and her purse fell on the floor. She and Doc bent down at

61

the same time to pick it up, and knocked heads.

"Oh, dear," said Mrs. Sparks, rubbing her fore-head. "First my daughter blacks your son's eye, then I almost knock you out! I'm terribly sorry. Are you all right?"

Doc rubbed his head, too, but he was grinning. "I'm perfectly fine. As Vallie will tell you, I have a pretty hard head. It would take more than a little bump to knock me out." He handed her her purse, then shook her hand. 'I'm glad to meet you. How's our patient?"

"He's not so good," Sparky said before her mother could reply. "He still won't eat, and he doesn't want to drink, either. But we've given him his medicine like you said."

"Suppose you bring him into the treatment room, and we'll take a look at him," Doc said. He led the way, and Val, Sparky, and her mother followed, Val carrying the cat carrier. It weighed a ton!

"Doctor Taylor, about Teddy . . ." Mrs. Sparks began, but Doc cut her short.

"First Charlie. Then Teddy. Vallie, take the cat out and put him on the table. I want to take his temperature and check him out again."

Val did as she was told. Lifting Charlie was like picking up a big, limp, fur-covered pillow. He didn't struggle or cling, just let himself be moved around as though he were a stuffed animal. Doc checked his temperature, then peered into the cat's eyes, ears, and down his throat, using his little penlight. "He's still running quite a fever," Doc said. "He seems somewhat less congested today, however." He paused, then said, "Mrs. Sparks, has Charlie had all his shots?"

"Oh, yes," Mrs. Sparks said. "Every year. Charlie's a member of the family — we care for him as though he were a person."

"He's a lot nicer than *some* people," Sparky muttered, and her mother gave her a little poke.

"What about a vaccination against feline leukemia virus?" Doc asked.

"Feline leukemia?" Mrs. Sparks echoed, and Sparky's round face paled under its sprinkling of freckles. "I — I don't think so. Oh, dear, I remember getting a postcard from our vet in York saying that a vaccine was available and that Charlie should be brought in for a shot, but things were awfully hectic just then, and. . . . Doctor, are you saying that's what Charlie has?"

Doc nodded. "I'm afraid so, Mrs. Sparks. The laboratory tests were positive."

"Charlie *is* gonna die," Sparky wailed. Tears began to roll down her cheeks. "Nobody gets better when they have leukemia! He's dying right now, isn't he, Doctor Taylor?"

"No, he's not," Val said firmly. "You heard what

Dad said — he's less congested today. See, Sparky, feline leukemia *is* very serious. It's a bad virus, because his entire system can be affected by it. But if a cat can hang in there and fight off the first infection he gets, he'll probably survive. And it may not look like Charlie's fighting, but he is, deep inside. If you hadn't called Animal Inn right away, he probably wouldn't have lasted. You did exactly the right thing. You probably saved his life!"

Sparky sniffled and rubbed her nose with the back of her hand. Mrs. Sparks rummaged in her handbag and pulled out a tissue. "Blow," she commanded. Sparky blew, then said in a trembly voice, "Are you sure? How do you know so much, anyway? You're only a kid!"

"Vallie may be young," Doc said, "but she's been helping me for years, and she's learned a great deal about animal health. She wants to be a vet when she's older, and in my opinion, she's going to be an excellent one. Everything she just told you is true. If Charlie continues to improve, chances are good that he'll recover."

"Honest?" Sparky whispered, big brown eyes glued to Doc's face.

"Honest," Doc said solemnly. "Now, what we have to do is to make sure we knock out all the other infections that are making him so miserable. I'm going to give Charlie another shot of antibiotic. Then I'll give you some little blue pills and some white ones — you'll have to drop them down his throat. Vallie will show you how. The blue pills are a different kind of antibiotic. He gets two blue ones three times a day, and one white one. The white ones are cortisone. Cortisone works wonders on cats. I'm also going to give you a tube of ointment to put in Charlie's eyes twice a day. It will clear up that cloudiness that makes them look kind of whitish-blue. Keep getting fluids into him, and offer him very bland food every now and then. He'll probably start getting hungry in a day or two."

As he spoke, Doc was putting pills into little plastic containers. Val went out to the reception desk to type up labels for the pills and the ointment. Then she fastened the proper labels to the proper containers and came back into the treatment room to demonstrate to Sparky and her mother how to give Charlie his medicine.

"It's real easy now, because he's not feeling good so he won't fight," she explained, tucking Charlie under her left arm. "As he gets better, it might take both of you to hold him down. What you do, see . . ." she gently squeezed both corners of Charlie's jaw with the fingers of her left hand until he was forced to open his mouth, then popped one of the little white pills down his throat with her right hand, ". . . is this," she finished. "Then you stroke him under the chin downward, to help him swallow the pill. That's all there is to it."

"I can do that," Sparky said.

"I'll help you, honey," Mrs. Sparks added.

Val then showed them how to squeeze a little dab of ointment in the corners of Charlie's eyes near his nose, and how to hold his eyelids closed until the ointment spread over the eyeballs. "You're a super patient, Charlie," she told the cat as she put him back into his carrier. "And you're going to be feeling much better in no time flat."

"You're *sure* he's gonna get well?" Sparky persisted, reaching into the cat carrier and stroking Charlie's thick gray fur.

"As sure as we can be," Doc told her, smiling. "As I told you yesterday, one of the most important medicines you can give a sick animal is love, and I can see that you have plenty of that to give. If he takes a turn for the worse — which I don't think he will — but just in case," he added quickly, "don't hesitate to call me either here at Animal Inn or at my home number. Vallie will write it down for you."

"Thank you so much, Doctor Taylor," Mrs. Sparks said, shaking Doc's hand again. "I guess you can tell how important Charlie is to Sparky. Our lives have been pretty — well, pretty messed up lately, for various reasons. . . ."

"I told Val about you and Dad getting divorced,

and us moving here and all," Sparky said.

"Oh." Mrs. Sparks sighed and shrugged. "I might have known. Well, then, perhaps you can understand why Sparky has had some trouble adjusting to her new school. I can't tell you how sorry I am about her fighting with your little boy. We've had a lot of serious talks, Philomena and I, about trying to get along with her classmates. She's not really a *bad* child, Doctor Taylor. Just lonely and confused, and a little scared."

"I am *not* scared!" Sparky said, scowling. "The other kids are scared of *me*, that's who's scared!" She paused. "Except Teddy. He's not scared of anything. That's why I have to keep beating him up."

"Oh, Philomena!" her mother groaned.

"The last time, he kicked me in the shins real good," Sparky added. "I have a big purple bruise, only not as purple as Teddy's eye. Wanna see?" She was about to roll up one leg of her jeans, but Mrs. Sparks stopped her.

"That won't be necessary," she said firmly.

Doc crouched down so he was eye-to-eye with Sparky. "You know, Sparky, I have an idea. See what you think of it." He glanced up at Val, then turned back to Sparky. "Tomorrow afternoon I'm taking Val, her friend Toby, Teddy, and Erin out to a farm to see some baby lambs. How'd you like to come along? If your mother says it's all right, that is."

"Uh . . . Dad . . ." Val began, trying frantically to think of some way to make him take back this surprising invitation. That would be all they'd need — Teddy and Sparky at each other's throats all afternoon! What was Doc thinking of?

"It might be a good way for you and Teddy to get to know each other better," Doc continued, ignoring Val. "I happen to think my son's a pretty nice person, and I happen to think you are, too. I'd like to give you both a chance to find that out." He looked up at Mrs. Sparks. "What do you think, Mrs. Sparks? Are you willing to let Sparky spend the afternoon with me and my family? I promise I'll keep a close eye on her, and those twin lambs are pretty cute." He turned back to Sparky. "Ever see newborn lambs up close?"

Sparky shook her head. She was chewing on a pigtail again.

"Maybe Mrs. Sparks has something planned for tomorrow," Val said quickly.

But Sparky's mother didn't take the hint. "Actually, I was hoping to be able to finish unpacking," she said. "It would be pretty dull for Philomena. . . . Yes, Doctor Taylor, I think it would be fine for her to go with you. I agree that it might help to smooth things over between her and Teddy."

"Aw, Mom, I don't wanna spend a whole afternoon with Terrible Teddy," Sparky mumbled around the pigtail end. Her mother twitched it out of her mouth. "Besides, I have to stay home and take care of Charlie."

"I'm perfectly capable of taking care of Charlie for a few hours," Mrs. Sparks told her. "It will do you good to get out in the nice fresh air and run around on a farm. Thank you very much, Doctor Taylor. I assure you that Philomena will be on her best behavior — won't you, dear?"

"I will if *he* will," Sparky said.

"He will," Doc assured her. "Val and I will see to it, right, Vallie?"

"I guess so," Val sighed. Great. Just what she'd always wanted — to play nursemaid to two feisty little kids.

"We'll pick Sparky up around one o'clock tomorrow afternoon," Doc said. "Now, Vallie, if you'll wash down the treatment table with disinfectant, I'll ask Toby to send in the next patient."

Chapter
6

"No way! Not on your life! Uh-uh! Not in a million years!"

Doc had just told Teddy and Erin about Sparky's cat, and had announced that Sparky would be joining them on their expedition to the Bauers' farm. Teddy was having none of it.

"You'll have to tie me up with *ropes* and *drag* me," he shouted at the top of his lungs. "I've told you and *told* you — I hate that kid! She's mean and sneaky, and she doesn't fight fair, and — and I hope her old cat *dies*, so there!"

"Teddy!" Val gasped. "Take that back! What an awful thing to say!"

"Yes, Teddy, that's *really* nasty," Erin added, shocked. "Just because you don't like Sparky is no reason for you to want her poor sick cat to die." Erin paused, then said, "Philomena. That's such a pretty name. It's so dainty. If my name was Philomena, I wouldn't want to be called Phil, or Sparky. Sparky sounds like a dog's name."

"I think it's a perfect name for her," Teddy growled. "Philomena. She's mean all right! She's meaner than a junkyard dog. Sorry, guys," he said to Jocko and Sunshine, who were listening to the conversation, tails wagging. "I shouldn't have said that. Dogs are a lot nicer than that kid! *Dracula's* nicer!"

"Teddy, you have made your point," said Doc. He was not smiling. "And I hope I have made mine. When we go to the Bauers' farm tomorrow afternoon, Sparky — or Phil, or Philomena — is going with us. She's a very unhappy little girl who needs to make friends. I know, I know," he said, holding up a hand to prevent another outburst from Teddy, "she hasn't exactly been going about it in the best possible way. And I don't like the fact that she keeps beating you up anymore than you do. But the fact remains that Sparky needs help, and I think we can give it to her. Besides, her mother needs some time to herself. They haven't really settled in yet. Think of it as your cub scout good deed for the day — make that the *month*."

Teddy pulled his Phillies baseball cap further down over his eyes and scrunched down on the sofa until he was practically flat on his back. He glared at Val from under the visor.

"I bet you laughed when you found out Sparky was a girl, didn't you?" he said.

"I did not. I didn't even smile, did I, Dad?" Val

said indignantly. "I was too worried about her cat to do much smiling. I don't see why you're so bent out of shape. What's the big deal? Personally, I'm in favor of equal rights for women."

"Vallie, I think that's a little farfetched," Doc said, trying to hide his amusement. "Equal rights don't extend to the punching out of one's classmates, no matter if they're male or female. Now as far as I'm concerned, this discussion is over. We're going to the Bauers' and Sparky is going with us. And I expect you to behave yourself, Teddy, and I mean it — or else — "

"All right. I'll behave — if *she* does. But if she starts anything, I'll punch her lights out!" Teddy stood up. "C'mon, Jocko, Sunshine. Let's go for your walk. There's a Disney movie on TV in a couple of minutes and I want to see it, so let's make tracks."

He clipped the dogs' leashes onto their collars and dashed out the door behind them like the sturdy little tail of a two-part kite.

Val looked after him, shaking her head. "I don't know, Dad," she said. "I hate to say it, but I don't think this is a very good idea. They really don't like each other. I just don't think it's going to work."

"I never said they'd become best friends in the course of one afternoon," Doc told her. "But at least they'll get to know each other better. Right now they're enemies who don't have the faintest idea what kind of person the other one is. By the time we get home tomorrow, they'll have had a chance to find out. Maybe what they'll find out is that they know each other better and they *still* don't like each other. Then again, maybe they'll find they have something in common."

"They already do," Erin said, grinning. "What they have in common is, they hate each other!"

Val gave her sister a look. "Cute, Erin, real cute," she said dryly. "Come on — let's go feed the rabbits and Archie and the chickens."

"I wonder what the Bauers' niece is like," Erin said as she followed Val out back. "Gosh, I hope she isn't anything like Sparky! If she is, I'm not going to have much fun, either."

"I'm sure she isn't," Val said. "Dad told us she's afraid of animals, remember? And Sparky's not afraid of anything at all — except Charlie dying, that is."

"He isn't going to die, is he?" Erin asked anxiously. "Leukemia sounds so awful!"

"It is, but if a cat survives the first stage, it has a good chance of recovery," Val explained slowly. "With careful treatment and good care it can reject the virus and be a pretty healthy cat again."

"Good," said Erin with a sigh. "Gee, Vallie, I think it's neat that you know so much about sick animals. I just get all upset when I'm around them."

"That's okay," Val said. "You're going to be a

ballerina when you grow up, like Mom. Ballerinas don't have to worry about stuff like that."

Erin made a pirouette on her toes, stretching her arms out gracefully. "Thank goodness! When I'm a famous ballerina in New York City, if I have a pet and it gets sick, I'll just send for you, wherever you are, and you can take care of it."

"I'll be right here in Essex," Val said, smiling, "helping Dad with his practice."

"But don't you want to be famous, like that vet we see on TV who takes care of movie stars' pets? It would be so neat if we could both be famous."

Val shook her head. "We don't need *two* famous people in the family, Erin. All I want to do is stay here and help Dad with the animals. That's enough for me."

Erin's heart-shaped face was suddenly solemn. "It's not enough for me. I want to be the very best ballet dancer in the world — a *prima ballerina*. If I stay here in Essex, I can't be. I want to go to New York, Vallie. I want to be a *star*!"

Val felt a little chill run up her spine. She knew Erin meant every word she said. Val just hated to think of the family breaking up . . . but then, that wouldn't happen for years and years. Val didn't want to think about it.

"You dance over and feed Archie and the chickens. I'll take care of the rabbits," she said.

"You're shivering, Vallie. Are you cold?" Erin asked.

"Yeah, a little. Come on. Let's hurry. I want to see that Disney movie, too."

"Hop right in, Sparky," Doc said. It was Sunday afternoon, and Sparky had just come dawdling out of the house on Walnut Street, followed by Mrs. Sparks. Mrs. Sparks leaned down to kiss Sparky on the cheek, and said, "Now remember, honey, *best* behavior, right?"

Sparky nodded silently and climbed into the back of the van where Teddy and Erin were seated. Erin was careful to place herself between Teddy and Sparky.

"How's your cat?" Erin asked. "Daddy told us all about him. Is he doing all right? Oh — I'm Erin. I'm Teddy and Vallie's sister."

"Hi, Erin. Yeah, he's doing okay," Sparky said. "He even ate a little piece of chicken breast this morning." She didn't look at Teddy.

"Hey, that's fantastic!" Val said, leaning over the front seat. " 'Bye, Mrs. Sparks. We'll have Sparky home in time for supper."

Mrs. Sparks waved, and Val, Doc, and Erin waved back. Sparky just huddled in the corner next to the door as the van pulled away.

"I like those little balls on your pigtails," Erin said brightly. "Purple's my favorite color."

"Thanks," Sparky muttered, staring down at her sneakers. She was wearing a purple-and-white striped T-shirt and a pair of obviously new jeans.

"I'm glad to hear that Charlie's eating," Doc said. "That's a very good sign. You and your mother are obviously taking excellent care of him."

"Yep," said Sparky.

Silence.

"Teddy, aren't you going to say hello to Sparky?" Doc said at last, glancing back at his son in the rearview mirror.

Silence.

Then, "Hi, *Philomena*," Teddy said.

"I hate that name!" Sparky snapped. "Call me Sparky — *Theodore*."

"Don't call me Theodore!" Teddy snapped back.

"What's the matter with Theodore?" Doc asked. "It's my name, too. I kind of like it."

"I don't like it when *she* says it," Teddy said.

"I think Philomena's a beautiful name," Erin said quickly. "I never knew anybody named Philomena before."

"Yes, it *is* a pretty name," Val said.

Silence.

"We're picking up Toby Curran at his farm," Val said, keeping her voice bright and cheerful. "Toby works at Animal Inn, too. You saw him yesterday, remember?"

"The boy with the big ears who was sitting at the reception desk? Yeah, I remember him," Sparky said.

Silence.

"Toby doesn't have big ears. They're not any bigger than yours," Teddy mumbled.

"I do not have big ears!"

"No, you don't. Teddy, shut up!" Val said.

"She does, too! She looks like Dumbo!"

"Teddy, be quiet!" Doc ordered.

"I wanna go home," Sparky whispered.

Erin came to the rescue. "Tell me all about Charlie," she said. "Vallie says he's as big as Cleveland — that's our cat. Only he's mostly Vallie's cat. He loves her best. How old is Charlie? What does he look like?"

Sparky perked up a little. "Well, he's eight years old, the same as me. And he's gray mostly, only he has a white nose and chin and four white socks. He's my best friend. He's never been sick before, not ever in his whole life. But then, the other day when he got real sick, Mrs. Wilson — that's our house-keeper — told me to call Animal Inn, so I did, and. . . ."

She babbled on about Charlie and Erin listened with great interest. Val began to relax a little. At least Sparky and Teddy weren't going to come to blows during the drive to the Bauers' farm . . . she hoped.

Toby was waiting for them at the end of the road that led to the Currans' dairy farm, right next to the mailbox. He greeted everyone cheerfully, then asked Sparky how Charlie was, so Sparky started the whole story all over again. By the time they reached the Bauers' farm, everybody was chattering happily, except Sparky and Teddy. Teddy hadn't said a single word, and Sparky pretended he wasn't there.

"Here we are," Doc said, easing the van into the road that led to the Bauers' farmhouse. It was a big old sandstone house surrounded by tall trees. There was a large pond nearby in which a mother duck followed by six babies was swimming.

"Oh, look at the adorable ducklings!" Erin cried.

"They look just like Archie used to before he got all grown up," Val said, smiling. "He was such a cute, fuzzy little thing."

Mr. and Mrs. Bauer came out of the house, smiling and waving. They were both tall and thin, and sunburned even though it was only April. Behind them came a young girl whose long, dark hair was pulled back from her face in a ponytail. She was wearing jeans, and a bright pink T-shirt that said "New York City Ballet" across the front.

Erin grabbed Val's arm. "Look what she's wearing! And see the way she walks, with her feet kind of turned out? I just bet she's a ballet dancer, too! That must be Mrs. Bauer's niece."

"Come on, everybody," Doc said. "Let's get out and say hello."

So they did, and everyone exchanged greetings.

"Glad you could come, Doc," said Mr. Bauer, shaking his hand. "Hi, Vallie. Missed you the other day when your dad came over to help our Flossie with her twins. But Toby here did a fine job." Toby's ears turned pink with pleasure.

"I'm sorry I couldn't come, Mr. Bauer," Val said. "I can't wait to see them!"

"They doing all right, Mr. Bauer?" Toby asked.

"Sure are. We'll take a look at them in a minute," Mrs. Bauer said. "Now let me see — this must be Erin, am I right?" she added, and Erin nodded.

"How do you do, Mrs. Bauer? Thanks for letting us all come over today," Erin said.

"You're more than welcome. It's good to have a flock of young people around for a change. Marcy here gets pretty lonely sometimes, don't you, dear?" said Mrs. Bauer, putting her arm around the dark-haired girl's shoulders. "This is my youngest sister's child, Marcy Butler. Marcy, say hello to Erin."

"Hello," Marcy said in a voice that was barely more than a whisper.

"Hi, Marcy," Erin said. "I couldn't help noticing your T-shirt. Are you a ballet dancer? I am — I study with Miss Tamara in Essex."

"Erin's really good, too," Val said. "Our mother

79

used to dance with the Pennsylvania Ballet."

"Yes, I dance," Marcy said in the same soft, breathy voice. "Or I used to, back in Pittsburgh. I haven't danced at all since I came to stay with Aunt Edna and Uncle Fred."

"Then you two girls'll have a lot to talk about, I'm sure," Mrs. Bauer said. She gave Marcy a gentle little push. "Why don't you take Erin up to your room and show her your scrapbook?" She beamed with pride. "Marcy's got lots of pictures of herself doing all kinds of dancing. Run along, honey. We'll call you when we go see the lambs."

Marcy obediently headed for the house, and after a moment's hesitation, Erin followed.

"Well, now who're these two?" Mr. Bauer asked, looking at Teddy and Sparky, who were standing on either side of Doc. Both were wearing identical sullen expressions. "Knew you had a boy, Doc, but who's the little girl?"

"This is my son, Teddy," Doc said, resting a hand on Teddy's shoulder.

"Smile, Teddy, and say hello," Val hissed, giving him a poke.

" 'Lo," Teddy muttered.

"And this," Doc said, resting his other hand on Sparky's head, "is one of Teddy's classmates, Philomena Sparks."

"Call me Sparky," Sparky said.

"Sparky. Now isn't that a cute nickname," said Mrs. Bauer, beaming. "Nice to meet you both. Glad you brought your little friend along, Teddy."

"She's not my friend," Teddy said quickly. "We're in the same class, that's all."

Val rolled her eyes in exasperation. This was going to be a disaster, all right! "Sparky's new in town," she said, pasting on a smile. "She hasn't had time to make friends yet."

"Yeah, but she's had time to make a lot of enemies," Teddy said.

"That's enough, Teddy," Doc snapped, tightening his grip on Teddy's shoulder. Teddy winced, glaring at Sparky. Behind Doc's back, Sparky stuck out her tongue at him.

"Tell you what, Teddy," Mr. Bauer said. "How's about you and Sparky here taking a walk with Mrs. Bauer down by the pond? She'll show you where some duck nests are, and maybe you'll find some eggs. Didn't have time to look for them before. I dearly love a nice duck egg for my breakfast."

"Come on, kids," Mrs. Bauer said cheerfully. "Follow me."

Feet dragging, Teddy and Sparky trudged after her toward the pond.

"And you come with me, Doc," said Mr. Bauer. "You, too, Vallie, Toby. Got something to show you. Been clearing out the underbrush on that wooded acre next to the house, and it's looking real nice. Rigged up a swing from the branch of one of those big old trees 'specially for Marcy, but she's not much of a one for swinging." He glanced at Val. "You like to swing Vallie?" he asked, his blue eyes twinkling.

"You bet," Val replied with more enthusiasm than she felt. Swinging sounded pretty babyish, but she wanted to be polite. "And then can we see Flossie and her twins?"

"Sure can. Now, Doc, let me show you how I diverted the path of that underground spring so it runs right down next to the road. . . ."

Val and Toby trotted along beside Doc and Mr. Bauer, listening with half an ear to their conversation, and exclaiming politely over the bridge Mr. Bauer had built over part of the stream. Then Mr. Bauer led them up a wooded hill and stopped in front of an immensely tall tree where a wooden board hung from two ropes. Val looked up, up, up. The ropes were secured to a branch so far overhead that it seemed miles high.

"Wow!" Toby said. "How'd you tie that up there?"

"Extension ladder," Mr. Bauer told him. "Forty feet up. Want to give it a try, Vallie?"

"Sure," Val said, and sat on the swing. "Give me a push, Toby."

"Here you go!" Toby said, pulling her back and then thrusting her forward.

Val gasped as she swung out over the slope, almost to the road, and back. "It's like flying!" she cried. "What a great swing!" Back and forth she swung, propelled by hefty pushes from Toby. At last she called over her shoulder, "Want to take a turn?"

"Yeah, I wouldn't mind," Toby said. They switched places, and Val gave him a push with all her might.

"Hey, neat!" Toby yelled. "This is super!"

"I really thought Marcy would like it," Mr. Bauer said, a little sadly, Val thought. "But she's a city kid. She's afraid if she comes out here, she'll get bit by a snake or something." He sighed. "Marcy's got a lot on her mind. Her dad's been real sick, so Edna's sister sent her to us for a while. Marcy doesn't much like country life, I guess. Only thing she's interested in is her toe-dancing, and they don't have ballet lessons in the Consolidated School."

"Hey, Dad, guess what?" It was Teddy, running up the hill, Sparky at his heels. "I found three duck eggs! Sparky only found two!"

"Yeah, but mine were bigger," Sparky panted.

"Not *much* bigger," Teddy said. "You'll have lots of duck eggs for breakfast, Mr. Bauer — Hey, what a neat swing! Can I have a turn, Toby?"

"Sure. Hop on," Toby said, getting off and holding the seat steady so Teddy could climb on. "Hang on tight. Here goes!" He gave Teddy a big push, and Teddy soared out over the little valley. "Wowee! Vallie, look at me! I'm flying!" he shouted.

"You always wanted to be an astronaut," Val called back. "Get to know how it feels!"

"Me next! Me next!" Sparky cried. "C'mon, Teddy, don't be a pig. Let me have a turn."

"In a minute. I'm not through yet." Teddy squeezed his eyes shut. "I'm passing Mercury now, and here comes Jupiter! And there's a brand new planet over there, right next to Venus! Beam me up, Scotty — there's no intelligent life out here!"

Sparky giggled, the first little-girl giggle Val had ever heard out of her. Then she clapped her hand over her mouth and pretended she hadn't laughed.

"He's acting real silly," Sparky said, but her eyes were shining. "Y'know, I want to be an astronaut, too," she told Val. "Girls can be astronauts. Make him let me have a turn!"

Val laughed. "Let him come down to earth first, Sparky. Then you can have all the turns you want."

Chapter
7

When Teddy finally gave up the swing to Sparky, Val helped the little girl onto the seat, then pushed her for what felt like hours. But she didn't really mind, because for the first time since she'd met Sparky, the child seemed really happy. She shrieked with delight each time she swung out over the valley, and her round face was flushed with pleasure. At last Val's arms began to give out, and she said, "Sparky, wouldn't you like to see the lambs now? We're going to have to go home soon, and I don't know about you, but I'm dying to pay them a visit."

"Okay," Sparky said cheerfully. She jumped off the swing at the top of the slope. "Where are they?"

"Come on, I'll show you," Val said. Teddy, Toby, Doc, and Mr. Bauer had gone to the barn to take a look at Mr. Bauer's cows, so Val, with Sparky skipping along at her side, headed for the sheep pasture.

"You know something, Val?" Sparky said suddenly. "I haven't thought about Charlie at all. That's terrible, isn't it? I mean, him being so sick and all. I hope my mom remembered to give him his pills."

"I'm sure she did," Val told her. "And no, it's not terrible that you haven't been worrying about him. Worrying wouldn't make him get better any faster. And when you get home, you can tell him about everything you did today. It'll take his mind off his troubles."

Sparky gave her a skeptical look. "That's dumb. Cats don't understand people-talk."

"How do you know?" Val asked. "Don't you talk to Charlie sometimes?"

"Well, yeah, sometimes," Sparky admitted. "Only I'm not sure he knows what I'm saying. I wish he did. I wish I could talk cat-talk. I try, but when I say, 'meow, meow, meow,' I don't know what I'm saying. I wonder if Charlie does. Maybe I'm swearing at him, or something."

Val grinned. "I doubt it. I don't think cats swear much — except, come to think of it, my cat Cleveland swears at the dogs sometimes. But he doesn't say 'meow' then. More like 'grrr!' When we had the monkey, Cleveland used to swear all the time."

"A monkey? You had a *monkey*?" Sparky asked, her brown eyes widening. "How come?"

So Val told her about rescuing Gigi, the sick little monkey, from Mr. Zefferelli's carnival, and about Little Leo, the lion cub. Sparky was fascinated.

As they passed the farmhouse, Mrs. Bauer stuck her head out the door.

"Going to see Flossie's lambs?" she called.

"That's right," Val called back.

"I'll tell Marcy and Erin," Mrs. Bauer said. "They've been up there in Marcy's room long enough. That child never gets enough fresh air and sunshine."

She disappeared into the house, and a moment later, Erin and Marcy came out.

"Guess what, Vallie!" Erin cried, running over to Val. "Marcy's a *real* dancer! She's danced with the Three Rivers Ballet in Pittsburgh. You should see the pictures!"

"Gee, that's great," Val said.

"I love to dance," Marcy said simply. "It's the only thing I ever want to do — like Erin. Uncle Fred fixed up a barre for me in the basement so I can do my exercises, but it's not the same thing." She sighed. "Uncle Fred and Aunt Edna are awfully good to me, but I'd really like to go home. I worry about my dad all the time."

"Well, it won't do any good, so you might as well stop worrying, right, Val?" Sparky said. "I bet your mom's taking real good care of him, just like my mom's taking care of Charlie."

"Who's Charlie?" Marcy asked.

"He's my cat. He's got leukemia, but he's getting

better because Doctor Taylor and Val know just what to do for him. I bet your dad's doctor knows just what to do for him, too."

Marcy sighed again. "I sure hope so. I miss my folks a lot — and my dancing."

"But isn't it kind of fun, living on a farm?" asked Val. "I'd love to be surrounded by animals all the time."

"Vallie's an animal nut," Erin explained. "She's going to be a vet when she grows up, like Daddy."

"Animals scare me," Marcy confessed as the four girls walked toward the sheep pasture. "I've always lived in the city, so I don't know anything about farm animals. My aunt and uncle are trying to teach me about them, but I'm still frightened. I like birds, though."

"Your canary's beautiful," Erin said. "You'll have to come to our house and meet Dandy. He sings all the time."

"Caruso used to sing a lot," Marcy said sadly, "but he doesn't anymore. He's homesick, too."

"Caruso's a funny name," Spark said. "Why'd you call him that?"

"I named him after a very famous opera singer who lived a long time ago," Marcy said. She stopped at a wide metal gate and opened it, letting Val, Erin, and Sparky go ahead of her. "This is the sheep pasture." She came in, too, then latched the gate after her. "Flossie and the twins are over there, in that little pen," she said.

"Gee, look at all those sheep!" Sparky cried. "I want to pat them." She ran toward the flock of fluffy, black-faced sheep that had been peacefully grazing, but the minute they saw her, they all turned tail and ran in the opposite direction. "Hey, come back!" she called. "I'm not gonna hurt you. I just want to play."

"That's the way sheep are," Val said. "They're easily frightened. And when one starts to run, all the others do, too. Sheep aren't very smart."

"They smell funny, too," Marcy said, wrinkling her nose. "*All* farm animals smell funny."

"I guess they think we smell funny, too," Val said patiently. "Come on, Sparky. You can pat Flossie and her babies. They won't run away because they're in the jug."

"In the *what*?" Erin asked.

"The jug. That's what that little pen is called," Val explained. "Don't ask me why — it just is." She led the way to the pen and peered inside — and caught her breath. "Oh, no!" she whispered.

"What's wrong, Vallie?" Erin asked, coming up beside her. She looked in, too, and gasped. "Oh, my goodness. What's the matter with the big sheep? Why's she lying down like that? Is she sick?"

"I'm afraid so," Val said. "Marcy, go get your

uncle and my dad — quick! Tell them Flossie's down and she looks bad."

"I'll go with you," Sparky said. "They went to the cow barn, with Teddy and Toby."

Marcy and Sparky ran off at top speed, and Val let herself into the pen. Erin stayed outside, looking anxiously over the fence. "The poor little lambs!" she said. "If their mother's sick, maybe they'll catch what she's got. And they're so cute!"

The twin lambs had frisked off into one corner of the pen when Val came in and stood there on their wobbly legs, twitching their woolly tails.

"How come their tails are so long?" Erin asked. "I thought sheep had short tails."

"Their tails are long when they're born," Val said, kneeling beside Flossie. "When they're a few weeks old, the farmer or the vet puts a tight elastic band around the tails a few inches down, and after a while the rest of the tail falls off. It doesn't hurt them a bit and short tails are easier to keep clean."

"Yuck!" said Erin, making a face. "What do you think is wrong with Flossie?"

"Don't know," Val said. "I'm going to see if she's able to stand up."

She tried to lift the big ewe to her feet, but Flossie didn't seem to have any strength in her legs at all, and she was having trouble breathing.

"Here come Daddy and Mr. Bauer," Erin said. Val stood up with a sigh of relief.

Doc and Mr. Bauer came into the pen. Sparky, Teddy, Toby, and Marcy joined Erin along the fence. Mr. Bauer fell to his knees beside Flossie, stroking her long black ears.

"Floss, old girl, what's the matter?" he asked softly. He looked up at Doc. "What do you think, Doc? Lambing sickness?"

Doc nodded. "Looks like it. Any signs of stiffness or trembling in the past few days?"

Mr. Bauer shook his head. "Nope, none. And I've kept a real close eye on her, too." He turned to Marcy. "Marcy, you notice anything funny about Flossie lately? One of Marcy's chores is to feed the sheep," he told Doc.

Marcy hesitated, then said, "This morning she was walking kind of funny, but I didn't think it meant anything so I didn't tell you. I guess I should have . . . I didn't know." Her eyes filled with tears. "I'm sorry, Uncle Fred."

"That's all right, honey," Mr. Bauer said gently. "No way you could have known. These things happen to ewes sometimes right after they give birth. It's nobody's fault."

"Good thing I happened to be here today," Doc said. "We'll take Flossie to Animal Inn right away, start her on calcium supplements. Provided she doesn't slip into a coma, she'll be fine."

"Hear that, Flossie?" Val said to the sheep. "Hang in there, girl, and stay awake."

Flossie gave a weak little "baaa" and tried to raise her head, then fell back, exhausted.

"If you take their mother away, what'll happen to the babies?" Teddy asked.

"We'll just have to take Flossie's place for a while," Mr. Bauer said. "They'll have to be bottle-fed around the clock. Marcy, you're going to have to help me, okay? The twins will need a lot of tender, loving care while Flossie's away."

"But . . . but I don't know how," Marcy said. "I don't know anything about baby animals. I don't even know anything about baby *people*! I'm the youngest in my family. I never even baby-sat for anybody."

"It's real simple," Val said. "While my dad and your uncle get Flossie into the van, I'll teach you how to handle them. Your uncle can show you how to give them their bottles."

Doc went off to get the van, Teddy and Sparky trotting at his heels. When they drove through the pasture gate, Doc turned the van around and backed up to the pen. Mr. Bauer and Toby picked Flossie up and carefully lifted her inside, laying her down on a soft bed of blankets that Teddy and Sparky had spread there. Flossie bleated faintly once or twice, and the lambs answered her, sounding worried.

"Come on, Marcy — come into the pen," Val said. Marcy edged through the gate, looking as worried as the lambs sounded. "They won't hurt you," Val told her. "They're just little babies. They're scared, and they're going to be lonely. They'll need someone to love them." She leaned down and picked up the nearest lamb. It didn't weigh more than a large puppy. It struggled a little, but Val spoke to it in a low, gentle voice, snuggling it close to her, and soon it calmed down. "Pat the little guy, Marcy," Val said. "He doesn't smell funny, and he's real soft and cuddly, just like a stuffed animal."

Marcy stretched out a hand and stroked the lamb's head. "He *is* soft," she said. "I never touched either of them before."

"Now pick up his brother — or sister," Val ordered. Marcy approached the other lamb, who bounded away from her, then backed itself into a corner, looking frightened.

"Don't be scared," Marcy said, moving slowly closer. "I'm not going to hurt you." She bent down and picked the lamb up very, very carefully. Four spindly little black legs flailed widly for a moment until Marcy managed to get them under control.

93

"Hold him tight," Val said, "so he feels safe. If he thinks you're going to drop him, he'll be frightened."

"There, there, baby," Marcy crooned, getting a firmer grip. "You're not going to fall. Everything's going to be all right."

The lamb relaxed in her arms and gently butted her chin with its nose. Marcy giggled. "Hey, cut that out! I'm supposed to be your friend, remember?"

Mr. Bauer came back from the van. When he saw Marcy holding the lamb, he smiled broadly. "That's the ticket, honey. You're doing just fine."

Val put her lamb down. "I wish I could take them both home with me," she said. "But I can see they're in good hands. Thanks for letting us come, Mr. Bauer."

Mr. Bauer turned to Erin. "Erin, you come out and visit Marcy again real soon, you hear?"

Erin nodded. "Thanks, Mr. Bauer. Maybe you'd let Marcy come see us one day soon? I could take her to ballet class with me next Saturday. I'm sure Miss Tamara wouldn't mind."

Marcy looked at her over the lamb's head. Her eyes were shining. "Really? Oh, Uncle Fred, could I?"

"Don't see why not," Mr. Bauer said.

"Super!" Erin cried. "I'll call you in a few days, Marcy, and we'll figure out when you can come —

maybe Friday after school, and then you could spend the whole weekend."

"Okay!" said Marcy, beaming. She picked up one of the lamb's forelegs and waved it in farewell. "Wave 'bye-bye, little fella," she said. "Gosh, I'll have to think of names for the two of you — unless you want to name them, Uncle Fred," she added.

"No, the pleasure's all yours," Mr. Bauer said. "Anything you want to call them is all right with me."

Val and Erin got into the van, and as Doc drove slowly out of the pasture, everybody waved and Marcy and Mr. Bauer waved back. Doc stopped the van in front of the farmhouse.

"We must say good-bye to Mrs. Bauer," he said. "But quickly, now. I want to start treating Flossie as soon as possible."

Just then Mrs. Bauer came out of the house carrying a huge plate of cookies. "You're not leaving already?" she said. She looked disappointed.

"Afraid so," Doc said. "Flossie's come down with lambing sickness and we have to get her to Animal Inn. Thanks for your hospitality, Edna."

"Well, thank you for coming — all of you," Mrs. Bauer said. "Come again real soon. Poor Flossie! I better get right down to the jug and see to the lambs."

"It's okay, Mrs. Bauer," Val said. "Marcy's helping Mr. Bauer with them."

"*Marcy?*" Mrs. Bauer repeated, astonished. "Imagine that!"

"Uh . . . Mrs. Bauer, those cookies sure look delicious," Teddy said, leaning out of the window of the van. "Lunch was a real long time ago. I'm starvin' like Marvin!"

"Teddy!" Val groaned. "Mind your manners!"

"What's the matter with me?" said Mrs. Bauer, laughing. "I was bringing these cookies out so everybody could have some, and I clean forgot. Here!" She thrust the plate through Teddy's open window. "You take them. There's plenty more where those came from. You can return the plate next time you come."

"Gee, thanks!" Teddy cried. "Wow — oatmeal raisin! They're my second favorite, next to peanut-butterscotch-chocolate chip. Sparky, keep your grubby paws off!"

"Teddy!" Val and Doc warned together.

"Well, all right. You can have *one*," Teddy said, scowling.

Everybody waved again, and the van moved off to a chorus of "Thank you" from everyone inside.

"You better step on it, Doc," Toby said from the back of the van where he was sitting with the sheep. "Flossie's breathing's getting worse and she's starting to shake. She doesn't look good at all."

"Seat belts fastened?" Doc asked, and everyone nodded. "Hold on tight — here we go!"

96

Chapter 8

"Is she still alive?" Erin asked nervously as Doc and Toby carried Flossie from the van into the Large Animal Clinic. "If she isn't, I don't want to look."

"She's alive," Doc assured her. "Come on, Toby, let's put her in the stall next to The Ghost."

Val ran ahead to open the stall door, then stood aside to let Doc and Toby enter with their burden. Flossie didn't move as they laid her down on the thick, sweet-smelling straw, but Val could see her chest heaving with short, panting breaths.

"Can I help, Dad?" she asked.

"Yes — keep the young ones occupied while I administer a calcium supplement," Doc said.

"Here you go, Doc." Mike Strickler appeared in the stall as if by magic — as if he really was the leprechaun he so much resembled, Val thought. "Saw you carrying the old girl in. Lambing sickness, right?" He handed Doc a bottle. "This'll help her get better. Funny how it happens to some ewes and not to others. It's like all the calcium in their bodies goes into their babies and they ain't got nothing left for themselves."

"Will Flossie's babies get sick, too?" Sparky asked, peering into the stall and trying to edge around Val.

"No, it's not contagious," Val said.

"I wanna see," Teddy said, coming in, too.

"No, Teddy. Out. You, too, Sparky. You'll just get Flossie all upset."

Val gently shoved them ahead of her and closed the stall door.

"Let's say hi to The Ghost," she suggested. "C'mon, gang — let's go."

"What ghost?" Sparky asked, hanging back. "What're you talking about?"

"*Our* ghost," Teddy said, grinning devilishly. "I forgot to tell you. Animal Inn's haunted by this *huge* gray ghost! If you don't watch out, it'll getcha!"

Sparky stopped in her tracks, looking at him through narrowed eyes. "I don't believe you, Teddy Taylor," she said. "There's no such thing as ghosts. And if there was, they wouldn't come out in the daytime. And if they did, I wouldn't be scared of them, so there!"

"Oh, yeah?" Teddy growled.

"Yeah!" Sparky shot back.

"Will you two please stop that?" Erin said. "*Honestly!* You're giving me a terrible headache."

Val decided to ignore all three of them, and

loped over to the pasture fence. Rather than opening the gate, she climbed up and over, giving a low, piercing whistle. The Ghost, who was all the way on the other side, munching the sweet spring grass, raised his head. His ears pricked forward, and he set off at a canter straight for Val, frisking like a young colt rather than the elderly gentleman he was. Laughing, Val ran to meet him and threw her arms around his neck. Then, grasping his halter, she led him over to the fence where Erin, Teddy, and Sparky were standing.

"Animal Inn *does* have a ghost, Sparky," she said. "A huge gray ghost. And here he is! This is my horse, and that's his name — The Gray Ghost. Isn't he beautiful?"

Teddy and Erin reached out to pat The Ghost, but Sparky drew back. Her freckles stood out like specks of brown paint against her suddenly pale face. Wide-eyed, she backed away.

"What's the matter?" Val asked. "Don't you like him?"

Sparky backed away, shaking her head. "No! I don't like him at all! I *hate* horses!"

"Really? You're kidding," Val said, amazed. "How can anyone hate horses? Especially a horse like The Ghost. He used to be a champion jumper, before he got cataracts in his eyes. He doesn't see very well, and he's kind of old — older than me —

but he's the most wonderful horse in the world. Go on, pat him, Sparky."

"No way!" Sparky folded her arms across her chest, still shaking her head. "I'm not gonna touch that horse."

Teddy turned to stare at her as though she'd suddenly grown a second head. "Boy, Sparky, you are something else. You're weird, you know that? I mean *weird*!"

"Okay, you don't have to touch him," Val said. She climbed back up on the fence, and slid effortlessly onto The Ghost's broad back. "I'm going to go for a bareback ride around the pasture." She nudged The Ghost with her heels, grasping his silver mane with one hand, and the horse started off across the pasture, tossing his handsome head. Teddy was right, Val thought. Sparky was weird, all right. Imagine anyone hating horses! That was even stranger than being *afraid* of animals, the way Marcy was. . . . *Afraid*. Was Sparky *afraid* of The Ghost? No, that was silly. Sparky wasn't afraid of anything. She was a tough little kid, the Terror of Jackson School. And yet the expression on Sparky's face was definitely one of fear. Val glanced back over her shoulder. Sparky was still standing in the same spot, and she was chewing on the end of one pigtail. Val leaned down and pressed a hand against The Ghost's satiny neck, causing him to turn and jog back to where Teddy and Erin stood.

As she and The Ghost came closer, Val saw Teddy jump down from the fence and go over to Sparky.

"You're scared!" she heard him say. "You're *scared* of The Ghost, aren't you? C'mon, Sparky, admit it!"

"I am not!" Sparky muttered around the end of her pigtail. "I'm not scared of anything, Teddy Taylor. I'm not scared of you, and I'm not scared of some dumb old blind horse. I just don't like horses, that's all."

"You *are* scared!"

Teddy grabbed Sparky's arm. "If you aren't, come over and pat him. Come on — I dare you."

"No!"

"I *double*-dare you!"

Sparky wrenched her arm out of Teddy's grip. "Double-dares go first. You touch me again, Teddy Taylor, and I'll break your face!"

"Oh, yeah?"

"Yeah!"

"Not again," Erin sighed.

"Teddy, Sparky, cut that out! I mean it," Val called from her perch on top of The Ghost.

Teddy reached out and yanked Sparky's pigtail

out of her mouth. "There! I touched you. What're you gonna do about it?"

"I'm gonna *murder* you!" Sparky yelled, and flew at him, fists flying. In seconds, she and Teddy were rolling in the grass, punching each other and pulling each other's hair. Val slipped off The Ghost's back and wriggled through the fence. She ran over to the two squirming, battling children and tried to latch onto an arm, a leg, anything to pull them apart.

"I'm going to get Daddy," Erin cried, running toward the Large Animal Clinic.

"Teddy, stop that!" Val shouted. "Sparky, quit it! *Oh!*"

A small, hard fist had connected with Val's nose. It hurt like crazy. Val clutched her nose with both hands and felt warm, sticky blood pouring out between her fingers.

"You little monsters!" she yelled. "Okay, kill each other! See if I care!"

She was dimly aware of a large figure looming over her, thrusting a big red bandanna under her nose. "Dad, make them stop," she mumbled, pressing the bandanna to her face.

"That's enough," she heard Doc say, and over the wad of bandanna she saw him grabbing Teddy's shoulder and Sparky's arm. "You two stop it, and I mean *now!*"

"She hit me first," Teddy hollered.

"He said I was scared," Sparky bellowed.

"You *are* scared! You're scared of horses! Scaredy-cat! Scaredy-cat!" Teddy shouted.

"That's it!" Doc said, loudly and firmly. "Not another word from either of you! Vallie, are you okay?"

"*I* think they're perfectly disgusting," Erin said with a sniff. "Vallie, what happened to your nose?"

Val mopped at her nose and managed to say, "One of those little beasts socked me."

"Oh, dear," said Erin. "Which one?"

"I don't know," Val mumbled into the bandanna. "And I don't care. You're right, Erin. They're both absolutely disgusting!"

"Teddy, you sit down over here," Doc said, taking Teddy's hand and leading him away from Sparky. "And Sparky, you sit down over there." He took Sparky's hand and sat her down, too. Then he went over to Val. "Still bleeding?" he asked gently.

Val removed the bandanna briefly, then put it back. "A little. Not much, though."

"Erin, go get some ice from the refrigerator in the treatment room," Doc said. "Mike will unlock the door."

Erin ran off obediently. "I'll be right back," she called. Val nodded. She heard muffled sobs from both Teddy and Sparky.

"I w-w-want my mother," Sparky wailed.

"So do I," Teddy moaned, so softly that Val could hardly hear him. It wrenched her heart. Still holding the bandanna to her nose, she went over to him and sat down on the grass next to him, putting her arm around his shaking shoulders.

"It was me that hit you in the nose, Vallie," Teddy said, burying his face in her shoulder. "It was an accident. I didn't mean to hurt you, honest. I was aiming at *her* nose!"

"It's okay, Teddy," Val soothed. "It's not broken or anything."

"I wanna go home," Sparky mumbled.

"And you will, very soon," Doc said. He sat down next to Sparky and put his arm around her. "But you have to stop crying first."

Both Sparky's and Teddy's sobs began to subside into hiccups and little sad noises.

"I *am* scared of horses," Sparky said at last between hiccups. "They're so *big*! And when I was real little, I rode this pony, and he ran away, and I fell off and broke my arm. It hurt something awful! And horses are so much bigger than ponies. . . ."

"The Ghost's real gentle," Val said over Teddy's head. "He wouldn't hurt a fly."

Erin skidded to a stop beside her and handed Val a plastic bag of ice cubes. "Here, Vallie. Put the ice on your nose. That'll stop the bleeding," she said.

"Thanks." Val picked up the bag and held it to her face. It felt good. The pain was gradually going away.

"Have a cookie," Erin added, thrusting Mrs. Bauer's plate at Val. "I stopped by the van on my way back."

"Thanks," Val said again, taking one. "How about offering some to Teddy and Sparky, and Dad?"

"Well. . . ." Erin eyed the two children and her father. "Here, Daddy. *You* deserve a cookie."

Doc took two and offered one to Sparky. "Cookie?" he asked, smiling.

Sparky gulped. "Okay," she whispered, taking it.

"Can't I have one?" Teddy asked in a small, choked voice.

"Erin, give him a cookie," Val said.

Erin stuck the plate under Teddy's nose. He took just one and shoved it into his mouth. "Thank you, Erin," he said through a mouthful of cookie crumbs.

"You're welcome, I guess," Erin said, taking one herself and sitting down between Val and Doc.

Everybody sat and munched silently. Then Val heard The Ghost snorting and whickering low in his throat. He was stretching his neck out over the fence looking hopeful. Val took a cookie from the plate and stood up to take it to him. Teddy scrunched over to Doc, who put his free arm around him. When The Ghost had eaten his cookie, Val came back and sat down on the grass.

"I think it's time for some apologies," Doc said at last, looking from Sparky to Teddy. "Teddy, you first."

"I already told Vallie I'm sorry I gave her a bloody nose," Teddy said.

"I heard," Doc said. "But you owe Sparky an apology, too."

Teddy frowned. "I do not! She started it."

"I did not. *He* did!" Sparky said indignantly. "I told him not to touch me, and he touched me, so I punched him."

Doc looked from one stubborn face to the other. "Do you know something? I don't care who started it. What I *do* care about is that it's finished, and it's not going to start again, not ever. Now listen to me very carefully, and do exactly what I say. I'm going to count to three, and then you are both, at the very same time, going to apologize to each other, and this is what you're going to say: 'I'm sorry I hit you, and I'm not going to fight with you anymore.' Think you can handle it?"

"Aw, Dad . . ." Teddy muttered, scuffing one sneaker in the grass.

"Gee whiz . . ." Sparky said, tucking the end of a pigtail in her mouth.

"Ready or not, here we go. One, two, *three*."

Teddy and Sparky looked at each other. They both took a deep breath, then said together, "I'm sorry I hit you, and I'm not going to fight with you anymore."

"Hooray!" Erin cried, clapping her hands. Val grinned under her ice bag.

"Now shake hands," Doc commanded.

With a sigh, Teddy stuck out a grubby hand. After a moment's hesitation, Sparky took it. They shook, then dropped each other's hands as though they were red hot.

"This calls for a celebration," Doc said. "Any of those cookies left?"

"Just a few," Val said, passing over the plate. "But save some for Toby. Where *is* Toby, anyway?"

"Here I am." Toby, who had just come from the Large Animal Clinic, dropped down on the grass beside Val. He took a couple of cookies. "Thanks, Val. These are pretty good — not as good as Mrs. Racer's though. . . . Hey, what happened to you?" He had just noticed the bag of ice that Val was still holding against her nose. "Did I miss something?"

"You sure did," Val said. "Teddy and Sparky got into a big fight, and I kind of ended up in the middle. Teddy gave me a bloody nose."

"But I didn't mean to," Teddy said, munching on a cookie.

"No, it was an accident," Val agreed. "Actually, he meant to hit Sparky. But the fight's all over now, and Teddy and Sparky are going to be friends — aren't you?"

"Well, maybe not *friends* exactly," Sparky said. "Just not enemies."

Teddy nodded. "Not *worst* enemies, anyway."

"That's good," Toby said. "Being enemies isn't any fun. What was the fight about?"

"Teddy said I was a scaredy-cat, so I beat him up."

"You didn't beat *me* up! I beat *you* up!"

"If you want to know the truth, *I'm* the one that got beat up," Val put in quickly. "But from now on, nobody's going to beat up anybody, right, guys?"

"Yeah, I guess," Teddy said, and Sparky nodded.

"You're a pretty good fighter, though," she added. "Next time you and Eric and Billy play *Star Wars* at recess, can I play, too?"

Teddy thought about that for a while, then said, "Maybe. If it's all right with them."

Sparky looked at him and smiled, twisting a pigtail around one finger. "They'll say it's all right if you tell them *you* want me to play," she said. Suddenly she was all girl, not a tough little tomboy. "You're the leader. They'll do what you say."

"Yeah, I guess I am," Teddy admittedly proudly.

"But you can't be Darth Vader all the time, understand? We all take turns. And because I *am* the leader, you have to do what I say, too."

"Well . . . okay," Sparky said at last. They grinned at each other.

Doc gave them each a hug, then stood up. "I don't know about you, but I'm getting chilly. And it looks like we're in for an April shower. Time to go home. Vallie, you better bring The Ghost into the barn. I just want to take another look at Flossie before we go."

"She looks better already," Toby said. "Mike's been talking to her, telling her not to worry about her kids."

"That's *lambs*, Toby," Val teased. "Kids are baby goats!"

"Ha, ha. Very funny," Toby said. "Come on, I'll help you get The Ghost. You better take it easy, or your nose will start bleeding again."

"Race you to the van!" Teddy shouted to Sparky, scrambling to his feet.

"No fair! You got a head start," Sparky cried.

"Bet I beat you both," Erin said. "Let's go — it's starting to rain!"

Chapter
9

The following Friday afternoon, Val got to Animal Inn later than usual. The Hamilton Raiders had just played their first softball game of the season and had beaten the Madison Wolverines six to two.

"How'd it go?" Toby asked as she came into the waiting room, pulling on a clean white lab coat over her Raiders shirt.

"Terrific! We slaughtered 'em," Val said happily. "I got two base hits and a home run. And the Wolverines were league champions last year."

"That's wonderful, Vallie," said Pat. "Doc said when you came in, you and Toby are supposed to give the patients in the Large Animal Clinic their medications. Then one of you will have to cover the desk here, because I have a beauty parlor appointment." She smiled almost shyly. "Today's my thirtieth wedding anniversary, and my husband's taking me out to dinner at the Casa Roma, so I have to look my best!"

"Gee, Pat, congratulations," Val said. "Thirty years! Wow."

"Yeah, Pat, congratulations," Toby added. "But I don't see why you have to go to the beauty parlor. You look pretty good to me."

Pat giggled like a little girl. "Toby Curran, you're just the sweetest thing!" she cried. "Now, here are the cards for the last few patients. Mrs. White and Fritzi are next, when Doc's finished with Mr. Bauman's Persian. Then it's Mr. Allison and Frou-frou, his French poodle. And last is Charlie Sparks. He's not here yet, but he has an appointment for four-forty-five."

"Okay, Pat. We can handle it," Val said, bending down to pat Fritzi White, a small, fat dachshund, as she and Toby headed outside for the Large Animal Clinic.

"How's Charlie doing these days?" Toby asked.

"Just fine," Val said. "Sparky gives us an update on his health every single day. Ever since she and Teddy made up, she's been hanging out with him, Eric, and Billy. She spends a lot of time at our house. She's really a nice little kid, once you get to know her."

Toby grinned. "I can't picture Teddy with a girl friend!"

Val gave him a poke. "Don't you dare say that to him, or he'll give *you* a bloody nose! He doesn't think of Sparky as a girl. Matter of fact, neither do I, most of the time. Only, the other day, Erin took Sparky to her room and showed her Elizabeth, Erin's favorite doll. Erin says she's too big to play with dolls anymore, so she thought maybe Sparky would like to play with her."

"I can't picture Sparky playing with dolls, either," Toby said.

"Neither could I. But I peeked in the door, and Sparky was tucking Elizabeth into Erin's little doll bed. I didn't say a word, because I was afraid she'd be embarrassed. Sparky doesn't think of herself as a girl, you see," Val explained. "I heard her telling Teddy that her father was disappointed she wasn't a boy, so he brought her up as though she was. Her mom's trying to help her act more feminine, but it isn't easy."

"Sometimes I forget *you're* a girl," Toby said cheerfully. "You know, come to think of it, I've never seen you in a skirt."

Val tossed her head. "And you probably never will, either! How could I ride The Ghost and mess around with pigs and sheep and sick pets in a dumb old skirt?"

"I guess. Speaking of pigs, let's give Porky Fletcher his medication first. I'll hold him down and you pour it down his throat," Toby suggested.

They went into the Large Animal Clinic and began their chores.

* * *

Mr. Allison was paying Frou-frou's bill when Erin came into the waiting room. Val looked up, surprised. Erin hardly ever came to Animal Inn during the week.

"What're you doing here?" she asked.

"Don't you remember? Mr. Bauer's dropping Marcy off here in a few minutes so she can spend the weekend with me and go to ballet class tomorrow," Erin said. "So I came out on the bus to meet her," Erin saw Frou-frou, and went over to pat her fuzzy topknot. "What a cute little dog!" she cried. "I love the pink bows on her ears."

Mr. Allison blushed. "None of my doing," he assured her. "My wife dolls her up like that. Paints her toenails, too, see? Don't see how any self-respecting dog puts up with nonsense like that."

"I think she's pretty," Erin said, and Frou-frou wagged her tail.

"I like *serious* dogs myself," said Mr. Allison. "Always wanted a German shepherd. No nonsense about *them*. Come on, Frou-frou. Time for walkies."

Frou-frou minced out behind him at the end of her pink leash, and behind Mr. Allison's back, Val mouthed to Erin, *"Walkies!"* Both girls dissolved into silent giggles.

Just then Teddy and Sparky burst in the door, followed by Mrs. Sparks with Charlie's cat carrier.

"What's so funny?" Teddy asked. "You laughing at that silly-looking dog?"

"Teddy, hush!" Val whispered, but Mr. Allison and Frou-frou were safely outside.

"I hope we're not late," said Mrs. Sparks. She put the carrier down on a bench. "We had a little problem with Charlie."

"He's not worse, is he?" Val asked anxiously.

"Oh, no. Quite the opposite," Mrs. Sparks said. "He's feeling so much better that we had to chase him all over the house before we caught him. He hates being stuffed into his carrier."

Yeeeow, Charlie said.

Sparky bent over and looked through the mesh-covered opening. "Don't worry, Charlie. This won't take long. Doc Taylor won't hurt you. He's the one who made you well, remember?" She glanced up at Val. "You know, Val, I think you're right. I think Charlie *does* understand what I say to him. He looks lots happier now."

"What did I tell you?" Val said, smiling. "I'll tell Dad you're here."

She pressed the intercom button and spoke to her father, and Doc came out of the treatment room right away.

"How's our patient?" he asked, tweaking one of Sparky's pigtails. "Still on the road to recovery?"

"Thanks to you, Doctor Taylor," Mrs. Sparks

said. "It's really miraculous. I was sure we were going to lose him."

"Me, too," Sparky said. "Only now he's going to live for years and years and years, aren't you, Charlie?"

Yeow, said Charlie.

"Well, let's bring him inside and give him the once-over," Doc suggested.

"Can I come, too, Dad?" Teddy asked.

"Sure. The more, the merrier," Doc replied. He saw Erin, and added, "Hi, honey. Waiting for Marcy?"

"That's right," Erin said. "She ought to be here any minute." She turned to Sparky. "Can I take a look at Charlie? I've never met him before."

Sparky introduced Erin to the cat and Erin said all the right things about how beautiful and healthy Charlie looked. Then Doc led the way into the treatment room. As the door closed behind them, Marcy came into the waiting room carrying a small suitcase and a dance bag. She smiled shyly at Erin and Val.

"Well, here I am," she said. "Uncle Fred just dropped me off."

"Super!" Erin said. "We're going to have lots of fun this weekend."

"How's Flossie?" Val asked. "And how are the babies?"

"Oh, Flossie's just fine," Marcy said. "When Uncle Fred brought her home on Wednesday, we thought maybe she wouldn't remember Mickey and Dickey, but she did, and they remembered her, too. I really liked taking care of them while she was gone. They're so little and cuddly. Too bad they have to grow up into big fat sheep.''

"Better that than lamb chops," Val said, making a face.

Marcy nodded. "Sure is. I told my mother and father all about them when I talked to them on the phone the other day. My dad's much better now. I'll be going home the end of the month. But Uncle Fred and Aunt Edna want me to come back this summer for a visit, and I think maybe I will. And maybe you can come to visit me in Pittsburgh, too," she said to Erin.

Erin beamed. "I'd like that. We could go to see the Three Rivers Ballet."

"Dad's examining Charlie Sparks in the treatment room," Val said. "That's Sparky's cat. He's the last patient of the day, so I'm going to turn on the answering machine and go say hello to my horse. Want to come?"

"You have your very own horse?" Marcy asked, impressed.

"She sure does," Erin said. "Leave your stuff here. The Ghost's a wonderful horse. You don't have to be afraid of him."

"Oh, I'm not afraid of animals anymore," Marcy

said, walking beside Erin as Val started out for the pasture. "Uncle Fred even showed me how to milk a cow *by hand*! Usually they use machines, but he wanted me to know how farmers used to do it in the old days."

"I milked a cow once," Val said. "It was fun, but the milk tasted funny. Warm, and kind of strange. I like it better ice cold, straight out of the refrigerator."

"Me, too," Marcy agreed.

The Ghost trotted over to them in response to Val's whistle, and the three girls patted him. Val had brought some carrots with her, so she, Erin, and Marcy fed them to him.

"I'm going to get his bridle from the barn," Val said when The Ghost had finished munching the last carrot. "I want to ride him a little before we go home."

"Could we have a ride, too?" Erin asked. "Just a couple of times around the pasture?"

"Why not? I'll be right back."

Val took off for the Large Animal Clinic, and returned a few minutes later with The Ghost's bridle. She took off his halter and slipped the bit into his mouth, buckling the strap and flipping the reins over his neck. Then she climbed up on the fence and lowered herself onto his back.

"Don't you use a saddle?" Marcy asked.

"Not when I'm only staying in the pasture," Val said. "Don't worry. When you and Erin ride, I'll lead him around. He's very gentle. You won't fall off."

She urged The Ghost into a canter, gripping tightly with her legs. Val loved riding bareback. It felt as though she was actually a part of the horse, like one of those mythical creatures she'd read about who were half human, half horse. That's me, she thought happily. I'm a centaur. Wouldn't it be neat if there really were creatures like that? But she knew there weren't, and that was all right, too. It was much more fun just being Val Taylor, riding her very own horse that she loved.

And, Val admitted to herself honestly, showing off just a little for Marcy's benefit! She pulled back gently on the reins, slowing The Ghost to a trot and then a walk, and ended up in front of Erin and Marcy.

Marcy's eyes were wide with admiration. "You're such a good rider, Val," she said. "You and The Ghost looked beautiful out there!"

That made Val feel good. "Thanks, Marcy. The Ghost's beautiful, all right. I don't know about me!" She slid down to the ground. "It's your turn now. Why don't you and Erin both get on?"

"Both at once?" Marcy asked. "Won't that be too much weight for him?"

Val laughed. "No way! Together, you two probably don't weigh as much as I do. The Ghost won't mind."

She moved the horse over closer to the fence,

and first Erin, then Marcy got onto his broad back. Marcy put her arms around Erin's waist, and Val began leading The Ghost around the pasture.

"Hey, Vallie, can I have a ride next?" It was Teddy, racing toward them from Animal Inn. Sparky was right behind him, but now she slowed down. Doc and Mrs. Sparks and Toby brought up the rear.

"Sure, just as soon as Erin and Marcy are through," Val told him.

"What a handsome horse!" said Mrs. Sparks.

"He's Vallie's," Teddy said proudly. "She bought him with her own money when his mean old owners were going to have him put to sleep."

Doc looked down at Sparky. "Wouldn't you like to have a ride, too?" he asked. But Sparky shook her head.

"I don't like horses," she said. "And don't you say anything, Teddy Taylor!"

Teddy put on his "innocent angel" expression. "Who, me? I wasn't gonna say a word. I wasn't gonna call you a scaredy-cat or anything like that."

"Teddy . . ." Doc warned.

"Okay, okay. I *said* I wasn't gonna say it," Teddy said.

"He looks very gentle to me, honey," Mrs. Sparks said, resting a hand on Sparky's shoulder. "Erin and Marcy seem to be having a lovely time."

"He *is* gentle," Toby said. "Val lets me ride him

119

sometimes. There's nothing to be scared of, Sparky."

"I'm *not* scared!" Sparky muttered, narrowing her eyes and glaring at Teddy.

Val led The Ghost back to the fence, and Toby climbed over and helped Erin and Marcy down.

"Okay, Teddy, your turn," Val said.

Teddy started over the fence, then looked down over his shoulder at Sparky. "Ladies first," he said with a grin.

But Sparky just stuck the end of a pigtail in her mouth and shook her head. Val handed The Ghost's reins to Toby and ducked under the fence. She went over to Sparky.

"How old were you when you fell off that pony, Sparky?" she asked.

"I think I was five — or maybe six," Sparky said. "A long time ago."

"That *was* a long time ago," Val said solemnly. "But do you know what they say you should do when you have a fall?"

Sparky shook her head again.

"They say you're supposed to get right back on, or else you'll always be scared. You couldn't get back on because you broke your arm. That's why you're afraid. If you ride The Ghost now, you won't be afraid anymore. And you won't fall off, I promise. I won't let you."

"I — I don't know. . . ." Sparky whispered. "He's awful high up."

"Yes, he is," Val agreed. "But look how wide his back is. You'd really have to work at falling off. Give it a try, Sparky."

"Yeah, try it," Teddy put in. "Horseback riding's fun."

But Sparky didn't budge.

Val sighed. She looked over at The Ghost, who was sticking his head between the fence rails watching her. "You know what, Sparky? I think you've hurt The Ghost's feelings. Nobody's ever been scared of him before. And he's never heard anybody say they don't like horses, either. He looks pretty sad to me. You don't want him to be sad, do you?"

"N-no," Sparky faltered.

"Then give it a try. If you don't like it, I'll take you right off, honest."

"If you do, I'll never call you a scaredy-cat again," Teddy promised.

Sparky squared her jaw and took the pigtail out of her mouth. "Okay," she said.

"That's my brave girl!" said Mrs. Sparks.

"I'll give you a boost," Doc said. Before Sparky could change her mind, he swung her up and over the fence, then lifted her onto The Ghost's back. Val showed her how to hold the reins.

"All set?" she asked.

"I-I guess so," Sparky answered faintly.

"Then let's go." Toby stepped aside, and Val began leading the horse very slowly across the pasture.

"Ride 'em, cowboy!" Teddy shouted.

"You look real good up there, honey," said Mrs. Sparks.

"See? Nothing to it," Val said, looking back at the little girl.

Slowly, Sparky began to relax. The tight, frightened expression on her face gave way to the shadow of a smile. The smile got bigger and bigger.

"Know what, Val?" she said. "I like it! I'm not scared anymore, not one bit . . . but don't let go of him, okay? I don't know how to drive him yet, and he might crash into the fence or something."

"I won't let go," Val promised, grinning.

Sparky leaned down and whispered, "Know something else, Val?"

"What?" Val whispered back.

"I like Teddy, too. He's my very first friend since we moved to Essex."

"I'm glad," Val said, then asked, "Why are we whispering?"

"Cause I don't want Teddy to hear. I don't want him to know I like him until he tells me he likes *me*," Sparky said earnestly. "Cause if he finds out, he'll tease me to death, and I'll have to beat him up again."

"I won't tell," Val said, smothering a giggle.

"Cross your heart and hope to die?"

Val nodded. "Cross my heart and hope to die."

Sparky beamed. "Good! Can you make The Ghost go a little faster? I want to show Teddy I'm a good rider."

As Val lengthened her stride, she was thinking that over the past week, the Taylor family had made a lot of new friends — Sparky and Mrs. Sparks and Charlie and Marcy and Flossie and the lambs.

"New friends are nice," she said aloud in The Ghost's ear, "but old friends are extra-special, like Toby and Jill and you. I love you, Ghost."

And The Ghost nodded his head and whuffled gently near her ear as though to say, "I love you, too."

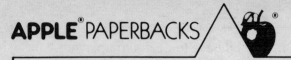
APPLE® PAPERBACKS

More books you'll love, filled with mystery, adventure, friendship, and fun!

NEW APPLE TITLES

☐ 40388-5	**Cassie Bowen Takes Witch Lessons**		$2.50
	Anna Grossnickle Hines		
☐ 33824-2	**Darci and the Dance Contest**	Martha Tolles	$2.50
☐ 40494-6	**The Little Gymnast**	Sheila Haigh	$2.50
☐ 40403-2	**A Secret Friend**	Marilyn Sachs	$2.50
☐ 40402-4	**The Truth About Mary Rose**	Marilyn Sachs	$2.50
☐ 40405-9	**Veronica Ganz**	Marilyn Sachs	$2.50

BEST-SELLING APPLE TITLES

☐ 33662-2	**Dede Takes Charge!**	Johanna Hurwitz	$2.50
☐ 41042-3	**The Dollhouse Murders**	Betty Ren Wright	$2.50
☐ 40755-4	**Ghosts Beneath Our Feet**	Betty Ren Wright	$2.50
☐ 40950-6	**The Girl With the Silver Eyes**	Willo Davis Roberts	$2.50
☐ 40605-1	**Help! I'm a Prisoner in the Library**	Eth Clifford	$2.50
☐ 40724-4	**Katie's Baby-sitting Job**	Martha Tolles	$2.50
☐ 40725-2	**Nothing's Fair in Fifth Grade**	Barthe DeClements	$2.50
☐ 40382-6	**Oh Honestly, Angela!**	Nancy K. Robinson	$2.50
☐ 33894-3	**The Secret of NIMH**	Robert C. O'Brien	$2.25
☐ 40180-7	**Sixth Grade Can Really Kill You**	Barthe DeClements	$2.50
☐ 40874-7	**Stage Fright**	Ann M. Martin	$2.50
☐ 40305-2	**Veronica the Show-off**	Nancy K. Robinson	$2.50
☐ 41224-8	**Who's Reading Darci's Diary?**	Martha Tolles	$2.50
☐ 41119-5	**Yours Till Niagara Falls, Abby**	Jane O'Connor	$2.50

Available wherever you buy books…or use the coupon below.

Scholastic Inc. P.O. Box 7502, 2932 E. McCarty Street, Jefferson City, MO 65102

Please send me the books I have checked above. I am enclosing $_____
(please add $1.00 to cover shipping and handling). Send check or money order-no cash or C.O.D.'s please.

Name_____

Address_____

City_____State/Zip_____

Please allow four to six weeks for delivery. Offer good in U.S.A. only. Sorry, mail order not available to residents of Canada.
Prices subject to change.   **APP987**